T E X T
APPEAL

TEXT APPEAL

New York Times Bestselling Author

LEXI RYAN

Cover (c) 2015 by Sarah Hansen, Okay Creations

Interior designed and formatted by

www.emtippettsbookdesigns.com

For Brian.
Thank you for believing.

CHAPTER
ONE

"Hello, my name is Riley, and I am addicted to sexy lingerie." Riley Carter steeled herself to walk past Fredrick's of Hollywood without spending next week's paycheck. She kept her stride long and even, moving along with the Miracle Mile crowd in the oppressive Las Vegas heat. With every step, disappointment crushed her internal lingerie junkie.

"Keep moving, Riley," she told herself. But then she made a tactical error. She glanced at the store's window and saw four big red letters dooming her to a month of tap water and peanut butter sandwiches: SALE.

The mother ship was calling her home.

Riley peeked over each shoulder, scanning the crowd for familiar faces before tucking her head and making a sharp right into the store.

"Senorita Carter," Javier, the doorman, said as she entered the store. "We've missed you. Where've you been?"

Heat blasted her cheeks. She'd failed in her attempts to break her slightly naughty and very secret little addiction. She had made some progress, though. It had been twenty-six days, two hours and—she glanced at her watch—five minutes since she'd fed her inner vixen. In that time, she hadn't bought a single bustier, teddy, or lacey panty. "It hasn't been that long," she said, but it had felt like an eternity. So what? She had a lingerie addiction. She lived in Sin City, where people came to feed old addictions—and find new ones. In comparison, lingerie was harmless—though an old-fashioned crack habit might have been cheaper.

"Big sale today," Javier was saying, but she'd already zeroed in on the sale racks, mentally calculating her budget.

To her right, a mannequin wore a black leather bustier with red piping and matching corset laces—not a sale item. She wondered if Chaz would approve of it—or of any of the hundreds of naughty-but-never-worn items in her collection. She imagined the leather hugging the underside of her breasts, leaving the tops exposed. She had a pair of red stilettos that would look fabulous with—

Focus, Riley!

She narrowed in on the deep discount sale bins. Thirty seconds later, she was elbow deep in thongs, garter belts, and crotchless panties.

She studied a vibrant pink pair of the last and bit her lip. Though her collection would put the famed Victoria and all of her secrets to shame, she'd yet to indulge in this particular variety of naughtiness. What was the point? Crotchless panties were for women who had illicit rendezvous in restaurant bathrooms or the backs of limos. They were for women whose boyfriends were so hot for them they couldn't wait the two-point-five seconds required for panty removal.

In short, they were for hoo-haws that saw more sex than a hotel room above a twenty-four-hour wedding chapel on the Strip.

Riley sighed and fingered the lace tie at the panty's hip. A smile curved her lips as she remembered the text Chaz sent her that morning.

I miss you. Are you available for dinner?

She hadn't gotten a chance to answer him before her cell had gone missing. Chaz was the kind of guy she'd always wanted. He was courteous and gracious, and her father loved him. Like Riley, Chaz worked for her father's empire: Carter Hotels and Entertainment. He understood the demands of the business.

"Black lace would be a better contrast against your fair skin," someone said behind her.

Riley jumped and dropped the panties. Cheeks ablaze, she looked up.

"But I like the style. I could definitely see you in something like that." Charlie Singleton—the face of professional poker—stood before her wearing Ray-Bans and a come-hither smile that made her insides do a little Snoopy dance. Eyes concealed by his ever-present shades, the only sign of his approving once-over was slight tilt of his head and the Machiavellian smile twisting his lips. Damn it all, but he made her skin tingle.

Riley's Inner Naughty Girl practically purred. *Charlie would like the black leather bustier.*

Of course he would. Charlie liked women—in clothes, in lingerie, out of clothes, out of lingerie. From what she'd seen, he didn't discriminate. Heck, he probably made eyes at the old ladies who took up residence in front of the slots at the Bellagio. It was his special talent. He made every woman feel like the only one in the room. Or, at least, the only one who mattered.

"I'm just…I'm just picking something up for my friend," she stammered.

Charlie's broad chest shook with his silent laugh. "Isn't that the excuse I'm supposed to use?"

Riley pulled her shoulders back and stuck out her chin. "No, I don't imagine you'd use an excuse at all. Instead, you'd tell me that you were looking for something skimpy for your latest supermodel conquest. Then you'd probably try to get me to help you pick it out."

He cocked his head, thoughtful, then, with a shrug, nodded. "I guess that's a fair assessment. So, we've covered that I'm only here because I'm a womanizing cad." His smile let her know he wasn't displeased by the conclusion. "What about you? Is this a secret side of Riley I've been missing out on?"

Good gracious! She needed Charlie Singleton knowing about her lingerie addiction like she needed a hole in the head.

With a sigh, Riley snuck a glance at the pink panties she'd dropped into the bin. Damn, Charlie! She was going to have to walk away empty-handed now. Her Inner Naughty Girl whimpered.

She shot Charlie a glare she hoped was withering.

He shook his head and pulled off his sunglasses, giving her a full view of his rarely revealed ice-blue eyes. She wished he'd put them back on.

Charlie had this unsettling habit of looking at her like she was a triple chocolate ice cream cone with a single drip running down the side—a look that worried her as much as it turned her on.

"I'm glad to see you, Riley," he said, flashing that signature smile again. "I've been thinking about you." He eyed the discount bin. "And I can't say I mind the circumstances."

She nodded, pretending that smile didn't turn her insides to goo, pretending part of her hadn't been counting down the days until next week's thirtieth annual Grand Escape Resort and Casino's National Poker Tournament. Since her father's hotel hosted the tournament, it meant guaranteed face time with Mr. Two-Scoop Sundae.

She liked to look at Charlie. She liked the way he looked at her. Liked the way her belly flip-flopped when he entered a room. What was the harm in that? It wasn't as though she planned to *do* anything about it.

"Have you seen your sister yet?" she asked, groping for a subject safer than lingerie or even why he might have been thinking about her. Riley's roommate, Lacey, was Charlie's sister. Charlie had moved to LA as a teen and still kept a home there, but he was in Vegas often enough for poker tournaments that he and his sister remained close.

Charlie shook his head. "Just got in."

And Fredrick's was his first stop? Further evidence that Charlie was capital B, capital N, Bad News. Riley sighed and stole a final glance at the panties. *Adieu, my friend. We could have been great together.* "Well, I'll let her know. I lost my phone this morning and she's meeting me to help me pick out a new one." In fact, she was supposed to be on her way right now. *Not* shopping for lingerie with Charlie No-Other-Man-Will-Ever-Measure-Up Singleton.

Charlie looped his finger under the ribbon of the panties he'd caught Riley holding. He lifted them from the bin. "On second thought," he murmured, "the vibrant pink would look good with your dark hair."

Riley covered her face. "Oh. My. God. You did not just say that."

"What?" He pulled away her hand.

"I don't want you thinking about my hair *down there*," she whispered.

Charlie chuckled. "Who said anything about *down there*?" He shifted his gaze to the panties and, upon spotting their special feature, broadened his smile. "Well, I'll be damned. You're a little kinky, aren't you?"

She slapped at his hand, trying to make him drop the offending panties. "They're not for me," she seethed. "I have a friend who… who…" What? Had a medical need for crotchless panties? Bluffing had never been Riley's strength. "She's getting married."

He cocked a brow. "Honey, married women don't wear panties like these. These are reserved for wild single chicks, or…" He studied her for a beat. Raised a brow. "…good girls with a secret naughty side?"

One of the saleswomen approached. "How are you today, Miss Carter? Is there anything we can get for you?"

Riley cringed. She wanted to peek at Charlie—did he notice the saleswoman calling her by name?—but she was too nervous. There were plenty of reasons they might know her…

"I saw you noticing the black leather bustier," the woman continued. "I'll be honest, I thought of you when it came in. I thought, 'Miss Carter would just *swoon* for this!' And I was right, wasn't I? We even have a matching red leather thong. I tucked back a set in your size so we wouldn't sell out before you made it in. I know how you like me to do that."

"Um…" Riley wished she could disappear. "No, thanks, I don't think that's what I'll be getting my *friend*." She risked a glance at Charlie.

The saleswoman frowned.

Charlie was studying Riley now, but at least that damn smirk was gone. "She'll take it," he said, never taking his eyes off Riley's face.

The saleswoman's smile returned. "Great," she said before bouncing away.

"I'm not going to let you buy me lingerie, Charlie," Riley said, but her eyes were glued to the bustier on display, and Inner Naughty Girl was damn near salivating over the thought of her next fix.

Time she accept the facts: if she was going to kick this addiction, she needed professional help—something she should have recognized around the time she'd nicknamed her secret wild side her ING.

"Don't be a spoilsport, Ry," Charlie said, his voice soft.

Riley chewed on her lip and tore her eyes away from the bustier to look at Charlie. ING purred again. Apparently she liked Charlie even more than she liked lingerie—precisely why she couldn't be trusted.

"I see the way you look at that bustier."

"It's fine leather craftsmanship," she said, forcing a shrug. "I appreciate the work."

With a smile, he lowered his voice. "Honey, look at me like you're looking at that get-up, and I'll buy you the whole damn store." He winked and her insides shimmied.

The rational part of her brain stepped forward, and she thumped him on the arm. "Stop coming on to me."

He cocked his head. "Why?"

"Because I'm…" That was a good question. Why?

Right. Chaz. *Remember Chaz*, she lectured herself. "I'm seeing someone."

"Ah," Charlie said, sliding his glasses back on and hiding those hypnotic blue eyes. "And you don't want to be thinking of me when you wear it for him?"

"No!"

"You won't think of me?"

"I won't wear it for him," she said through her teeth.

He raised a brow. "Because…he prefers satin?"

"I'm not going to wear it at all," she seethed. "Chaz doesn't need me to dress in outrageous lingerie. He's very…respectable."

Charlie wrinkled his nose. "I'm sorry. Do you want me to talk to him about that?"

"Why would I—? No!" Why did she always let him do this to her? All he had to do was walk in a room and she turned into a frazzled, driveling idiot.

And—more to the point—why did she seem to *enjoy* it?

Charlie strode to the counter where the saleswoman was ringing up the bustier.

Riley swallowed. She could practically feel the leather now. What would it hurt, really, letting him buy her a little something? They were friends. Wasn't that what friends did?

Where was her reasonable self when she needed her?

You left her out on the sidewalk, Riley, right next to your dignity.

Charlie pulled out his credit card, and Riley groped at the last thread of her willpower. "Don't waste your money."

His gaze traveled slowly up her body, inch by inch. Her thighs clenched and her nipples tightened. "Trust me, it's no waste," he said, his voice rough and low. "And if you ever need someone to wear it for—"

He didn't get a chance to finish, because the man behind them in line tapped him on the shoulder.

Saved by the tourist.

Charlie turned around. "Can I help you?"

"Hey, man, are you Charlie Singleton, the professional poker player?"

Charlie smiled and offered his hand. "I sure am."

The man pulled a rolled-up manila envelope from his back pocket and slapped it into Charlie's open palm. "Mr. Singleton, you've been served."

...

CHARLIE STAYED behind when Riley left Fredrick's. Only after she was gone did he turn back to the woman who'd rung up Riley's bustier. He gave her the sweetest smile he could muster, given the circumstances.

Her eyes drifted south…and landed on the manila envelope. If she was wondering what the hell he'd been served for, she could take a number. "Can I help you?"

"You sure can. I was hoping you could tell me where Angela Rollins' office is?"

It didn't take a genius to figure out Angela had set him up. Her voicemail had been so sweet, he should have guessed she covering something vile.

Hey, Charlie, it's Angela. Yeah, remember from high school? Good times! Listen, I was hoping to see you when you're in town for the tournament. I'm the manager at Fredrick's on the Miracle Mile. Stop by.

Such an innocent voicemail, and he'd been half excited about reliving some good old days with her. Apparently he'd forgotten Angela's middle name was *Manipulative*. He didn't know what he'd just been served with, but he knew he had Angela to thank.

"May I tell her who's asking?"

"Just say her old friend Charlie is here. I'm sure she'll want to see me."

The girl nodded and picked up her phone. "Ms. Rollins? A man by the name of Charlie is here to see you?" With a nod, she hung up the phone. "Follow me?"

The narrow hallway behind the front counter led to a small office with a placard reading, *Angela Rollins, Manager*. Go figure, she hadn't lied about everything.

"Come on in, Charlie," Angela called from behind a big mahogany desk. She was tall and lithe, just as he remembered her, but she had a little age on her face now, and cynicism showed in the features framed by her stick-straight black bob.

"What is this about?" he said, holding up the manila envelope.

She smirked. "I see they found you."

"And I suppose I have you to thank for that? What the hell, Angela? I haven't seen you in sixteen years and you call out of the blue and ask me to meet you at your store so you can have me *served*? And why the hell didn't you try a fucking phone call first?"

She pushed back from her desk and smoothed down her skirt. "My lawyer thought it would be best to let the courts handle this. Since they couldn't catch you at the hotel, thanks to the limited access to that fancy suite, we thought this might work just as well."

"And, what, may I ask, is this about?"

She picked up her purse and slung it over her shoulder. "Listen, I don't want this to be ugly. I just want it to be over. If you have any questions, you can call my lawyer." She handed him a slick beige business card and motioned him out of the office.

He begrudgingly stepped out and watched her as she locked up.

She turned around and ran her gaze over him—up, down, and slowly up again. "You look good, Charlie. I hope when this all settles, we can go for a drink and put this all behind us."

He watched her walk out the back exit before looking at the card in his hand.

CLERENCE FRENCH LAW, LTD.
Specializing in Child Custody, Child Support

TWO

Riley stared at her new phone and frowned. "I really don't think I needed anything this high tech." She opened the door to the apartment she and Lacey shared. Jaws, her Bichon-Poo, hopped off the couch and made a beeline for her.

Lacey laughed. "Ry, that's not high tech. It's just a standard smart phone."

Riley wrinkled her nose. She dropped her bags on the couch and crouched to greet the dog who instantly rolled on his back for a belly rub. "I don't need my phone to check my email. I have a computer for that."

"Your dog is such a man-whore," Lacey said.

Riley rubbed Jaws' tummy, and crooned, "She's so mean," but she didn't deny it. She looked up at Lacey. "I just think I need something simpler."

"It's pretty standard stuff these days. Did no one welcome you to the twenty-first century?" Lacey grinned. "Just wait. You're going to love having your work calendar sync right up with that puppy. Once you're Grand Escape's general manager, you'll love having your email at your fingertips."

Riley studied the phone again, a sleek little chrome number

the guy at the counter swore would be her new crack cocaine—was that supposed to be a selling point? "*If* I get the position. I had to put in an application like everyone else."

"You'll get it!" Lacey said, tossing her purse on the counter. "You'll be the best GM Grand Escape has ever had."

"I hope you're right," Riley muttered. She shook her head, trying to toss thoughts of work to the side. "I need to figure out how to program my numbers into this phone before dinner." She walked across the living room and pulled her address book from her desk, leaving Jaws behind to beg for attention from Lacey.

"Wow," Lacey said, pulling the ball of apricot fur into her arms. "I didn't know anyone still had one of those."

"Good thing I do."

"Yeah, I guess so. It's just a pain because if you hadn't lost your old phone, they could have synched them and loaded all your numbers into the new phone for you."

Riley shook her head. "If I hadn't lost my old phone, I wouldn't have bought the new phone."

Lacey rolled her eyes. "Ry, it was the size of my purse and it didn't even have a camera."

"I never had to worry about misplacing it." Riley frowned. "Until I did. And who the heck decided phones should double as cameras?"

"Someone who understood the hidden potential of phone sex. You *needed* to upgrade."

"Yeah, well, I guess it's good that today's trip to Fredrick's was on your brother," Riley mumbled.

"Here, give me that. I'll be able to program it way faster than—" She stopped and her big blue eyes rounded. "Wait. What did you just say?"

"I ran into Charlie at Fredrick's of Hollywood." Just talking about him made her lips tug into a grin. Dear God, she was pathetic.

"You did?"

"I know I said I wasn't going to shop there anymore, but they were having a *sale*, and—"

Lacey swatted her arm. "I don't care about why you were in there! A girl deserves pretty things."

Riley rolled her eyes. "I don't need a whole *closet* full of lingerie, though."

"Who cares? God knows if I were about to come into the amount of fat cash you are, I'd have twenty maxed-out credit cards and a different pair of panties for every day of the year. I want to know why *my brother* was buying you underwear!"

Riley ignored Lacey's assumption that she was even interested in the "fat cash." At thoughts of Charlie, she put her hand over her face. "Oh, God, it was embarrassing! And not underwear, no, nothing that innocuous."

"What'd he buy you?" Lacey's gaze shot to the nondescript, eco-friendly canvas shopping bag on the couch. "Is it in there?"

But before Riley could respond, Lacey was pulling out sexy, sexy leather and Riley's ING was squirming impatiently, saying, *Let me try it on. Now!*

Lacey's jaw dropped. "Oh. My. God. This is so hot." She laid it out on the back of the couch and looked at Riley. "Do I even *want* to know why my brother bought this for you?" She smiled. "Charlie's always been sweet on you. If he weren't my brother, I'd tell you to go act like the young woman you are and have a wild affair."

Riley thumped her friend's arm. "I'm with *Chaz*."

"What happens in Vegas stays in Vegas," Lacey said with a shrug.

"Yeah, but I have to live here." Riley looked at her watch. "Listen, speaking of Chaz, will you really program that for me? I'm going out with him tonight, and he gets irritated if I answer unimportant calls when we're together."

Lacey rolled her eyes. "What do you see in him, anyway?"

Riley shrugged, dropping the address book on the end table. "He's a nice guy." She headed for the bathroom to get ready.

Lacey scoffed. "Riley, hon, I love you, and if this is who you want to be with, I'll shut my mouth, but you seem awfully serious about this guy and you've never even played the field."

Riley plugged in her straightening iron to warm, then climbed into the shower. "What?"

"I'm afraid you're with Chaz for the wrong reasons," Lacey said over the sound of the spray.

Riley's jaw dropped. "Like what?" She peeked around the shower curtain.

Lacey was sitting on the bathroom counter, address book on her lap, cell phone in her hand. Riley had known Lacey since after college, when they'd both needed roommates to save a little cash. Shortly after they'd moved in together, Riley had gotten Lacey a job at the front desk of Grand Escape. Living and working together, the two bonded quickly, but never in all that time had Lacey said anything so blatantly disapproving of her relationship with Chaz. "How can you say that?"

Lacey shrugged. "Riley, he's your dad's favorite employee. Don't you think that influences your feelings for him more than a little?"

She closed the curtain again and shampooed her hair. "That's not fair. My father likes him, but that's not why *I* like him."

Riley could hear Lacey's dramatic sigh over the shower. She thought she heard her mumble, "I don't know why else you would."

Riley closed her eyes under the pounding water and sighed. Chaz was a good guy. He would make a good husband. A good partner in the successful life they both wanted. "I think you just don't know him as well as I do," she muttered, trying—and failing—to keep the pout out of her voice.

"You're probably right. Don't be upset. The stuff with Charlie just...had me thinking."

Riley turned off the water then grabbed a towel. She wouldn't be angry with Lacey, because Lacey had no way of knowing Chaz was so good to her. If anything, this was Riley's fault, because when she did talk to Lacey about her love life, it was usually to complain about the sex—something it was time she took into her own hands. She'd been complaining that things between her and Chaz were a little bland, but she had a spice cabinet, didn't she?

Chaz was a great catch and she'd be foolish to let him slip by.

Wrapping the towel under her arms, Riley stepped out of the shower.

"I'll get out of your way," Lacey said, hopping off the counter.

"He's good for me," Riley whispered when she was alone. *But what about me?* her Inner Naughty Girl asked. Riley sighed as she reached for her hairdryer and brush.

Her father was retiring at the end of the month. He would still be involved in making the major company decisions, but later this week he would announce whom he would leave in charge to be the general manager of Grand Escape. Riley hoped he would name her, and with Chaz by her side, they would eventually run Carter Hotels and Entertainment in a way that made her father proud.

Chunk by chunk, she dried her hair with a round brush, taming the dark curls with each stroke.

"There!" Lacey called from the living room. "Your phone is all programmed, and in record time, too. God, I'm good!"

"Thanks, Lacey," Riley said, taking the flat iron to her hair now. "I owe you one."

Sure, Chaz didn't make her heart pound like a certain poker player. But she didn't feel safe with guys like Charlie Singleton. She never knew what would happen next when she was around them. When she was with Chaz, she didn't have to worry about life spinning out of her control. She always knew what would happen next.

"I'm sorry for what I said about Chaz," Lacey said, strolling into the bathroom and placing Riley's phone on the sink. "I guess I just worry because I know you're not completely"—she smirked—"*satisfied* in that relationship."

In the mirror, Riley watched the blush seep into her cheeks. "I'm going to work on that. Don't worry about me."

Lacey twisted a lock of her blond hair, studying Riley. "Maybe you should send him a suggestive text. That should be gas on the fire."

Right. Chaz sexting. Riley couldn't see it, and raised an eyebrow to let Lacey know as much.

Lacey shrugged. "Just an idea," she said, turning to leave.

"Hey, Lace, do you know any reason Charlie would have been served with court papers?"

...

CHARLIE WATCHED his sister take a long drink of her red wine and ignored the pap member snapping pictures from the corner of the dimly lit restaurant. As soon as the asshole did a little fact-checking and discovered the long-legged blonde across the table was Charlie's sister, not his latest love interest, the pictures would go in the trash and Charlie would be old news again.

"What are you going to do?" Lacey asked.

"Call my lawyer?" The manila envelope had held a subpoena for paternity testing. *Paternity testing.* The words still made him flinch.

After sixteen years, Angela wanted to prove her child was Charlie's. Charlie didn't need to ask, "Why now?" He knew. Charlie had been a nobody when he and Angela had been fooling around. A nobody with no connections and no future. Apparently, winning a handful of national poker tourneys made him a *somebody* in Angela's eyes, and now—like everybody else he'd ever shared a meal with—she wanted a piece of his checking account. Would she have bothered if she'd known that checking account was rapidly dwindling, right alongside Charlie's future in professional poker?

"I don't really see what other options I have."

Lacey swatted his hand, making his beer slosh out of his glass. "Don't be a jerk, Charlie."

He slid his sunglasses down his nose and narrowed his eyes at her. "Excuse me?"

Lacey rolled her eyes. "Just because Angela wants to pull out the big guns doesn't mean you have to. What about the kid? What does he think about all this?"

"Hell if I know. Angela wasn't exactly forthcoming with information."

Lacey nodded. "Yeah, I remember her from high school. I never did know what you saw in her."

Charlie chuckled. "Long legs and sexual aptitude."

"Jesus. Real mature."

He lifted his hands. "What do you want? I was sixteen years old. I hadn't developed the depth of character I have today."

She snorted. "Speaking of your 'depth,' I saw what you bought my roommate. That was about as subtle as skywriting, Smooth. I suppose just asking her to dinner hadn't occurred to you?"

Charlie's lip twitched. "That stuff's for amateurs. I have skills that are much more effective than that old-fashioned crap."

Lacey didn't look convinced. She leaned back in her chair and crossed her arms, giving him a visual once-over. "Well, the outfit's hot, I'll give you that, but she still went out with her boy Chaz right after she got home, so I wouldn't be so sure of your 'skills.'"

"Yeah, she mentioned him. What's his story, anyway?"

"He's her daddy's golden boy. Like Riley, he assists Carter with running the hotels, but mostly he manages the string of sleazy clubs Carter owns."

Charlie raised a brow. "I heard the Black Diamond clubs were some of the classier in town."

Lacey snorted. "You can put lipstick on a pig, but it's still a strip club."

"So, this guy, he has Daddy's approval. How serious are they?"

"They're not engaged yet, but Riley's been seeing him for a couple years now. Personally, I think the only reason he hasn't popped the question is that he wants to fuck around, and that will be more difficult with a ring on his finger. Sooner or later, though, he's gonna ask. He's a lot less interested in Riley than he is in her trust fund."

Charlie shook his head. "I don't trust any man who doesn't like lingerie."

Lacey was silent for a beat, her attention on Tall, Dark, and Handsome at the bar. "So, what are you going to do?"

"It's too early to show my hand, but I'll pay to see the flop."

Lacey rolled her eyes. "In English, please?"

"Riley's cute, and if this guy hasn't made things official—especially if he's screwing around—"

"I don't know that for a fact."

Charlie shrugged. Lacey wasn't the type to indulge in idle gossip. If she suspected something, there was probably some truth to it—truth Charlie just might be able to bring to the surface. "I see no reason why I should back down," he said.

It'd be different if Riley weren't attracted to Charlie, but he knew that look she got in her eyes when he was around. He wasn't sure what kind of hand Chaz was holding, but if Riley's eyes on his body were any indication, *Charlie* was the one with pocket aces.

"Interesting. What about the kid?"

Shit. He didn't know.

A sour taste filled his mouth. He wouldn't let the kid be used as a pawn in some scheme. "I have money." *Some. For now.* "If I'm really the kid's father, she can have it."

Lacey leaned forward and glared at him. "Aren't you missing a possibility here?"

He frowned. "What's that?"

"You could be more than a sperm donor. You could be the boy's *dad.*"

...

"I HAD a fantastic time tonight," Chaz said, brushing a lock of hair from Riley's face.

She leaned against the stairwell wall outside her apartment, and his dark eyes met hers. Nice eyes—warm and comforting. But her mind drifted to a different set of eyes. Icy blue and dangerous eyes.

"It was nice," she murmured.

Stop thinking about Charlie! Maybe she was thinking about him because they had the same name: Charles. Charles Singleton and Charles Spencer—if her brain linked them, that was perfectly understandable, nothing to feel guilty about.

Chaz also looked a little like Charlie. They were both tall with dark hair and nice builds. She smiled at Chaz and gave him an appraising look. His body was good. It was…fine. But he looked about as much like Charlie as a veggie burger looked like the real, juicy thing. Sure, there were similarities, and at a quick glance one could be mistaken for the other. But the truth was, each promised an entirely different kind of experience.

"You keep looking at me like that and I won't make it home tonight," Chaz said with a smile.

"I'm just thinking about how much I enjoy being with you."

He leaned in for a kiss and she tilted her chin up and opened her mouth to him.

She wished his hint that he might stay over stirred something more in her. The truth was, Chaz wasn't a very exciting lover. He was practical and didn't stray off course. He was…efficient.

Charlie Singleton might make a girl wonder what he would do with his mouth, but this was Chaz. Chaz was kind. Honest. The kind of man you could be proud of. The kind of man you marry and want to father your children. He was successful and stable and…

He put his thumb under her chin and slipped his tongue into her mouth, tasting of mineral water and Juicy Fruit, and Riley thought, *He's lower in cholesterol.*

She giggled against his lips.

Chaz pulled away and frowned. "Something wrong?"

She bit her lip, trying to stop the laughter bubbling there, but it just kept spilling out. "My mind is somewhere else."

"Well, then."

Crap, now he was scowling. She was pretty sure making her date scowl at the door was not the way to add the spice she was looking for.

"Listen, I'm really sorry."

"It's fine," he said, but neither his tense shoulders nor his telling glance at his watch had her convinced.

"No, it's not. I'm sorry. Why don't you come in?" She opened the door but was too embarrassed to take her eyes off the floor.

Chaz cleared his throat. "Um, Riley?"

"What?" She followed his gaze to the couch…where her new leather bustier was nicely displayed. "Oh my God!" Her hand flew to her mouth. She had totally forgotten she'd left it there! What would Chaz think?

Behind her, he made an umphing sound she wasn't sure was good or bad. "Is that your roommate's?" he asked. "Of course it is. You wouldn't waste money on something so frivolous."

"Um." She spun around to face him. She had to think fast—but he was looking at his watch.

He smiled, but it was forced. "Listen, I should go. I have an early meeting tomorrow. I'll send you a text, though, okay?"

It was Riley's turn to force a smile. "Right. Okay, that'd be nice."

Chaz pressed a light kiss to her cheek. "I'll see you soon."

And as she walked him out, she couldn't help but think, *I bet Charlie Singleton doesn't end a date with his girlfriend with a kiss against her cheek.*

CHAPTER
THREE

Charlie studied the faces of the players around him. These were amateurs, cocky sons o' bitches who thought they could plop down at a Vegas poker table and take home a load of crisp new bills. Charlie wasn't interested in their money and carefully planned his strategy so he would win some, lose some, and walk away even-steven. He just needed some time with the game to stay loose for the tournament.

Located in a VIP private box, their game overlooked the stage where the illustrious Black Diamond dancers performed. The guy across from him signaled for another beer, and Charlie rolled his eyes. Too much alcohol could destroy the game of even the most experienced player, and yet when guys like this one wanted to "act like a pro," they drank too much and generally loosed up on all their good sense. Then again, people didn't come to the Black Diamond to practice self-restraint.

Charlie was lucky. Since he was fifteen, he'd had a talent for the game matched only by his passion for it. His and Lacey's dad had never been around, but a neighbor in the subsidized housing where he grew up had taught Charlie everything he knew about the game. He'd taught him how to deal. How to bluff. How to use deductive thinking to get a pretty good guess at what the other players were holding. But most importantly, Walter had taught him how to have fun without losing everything.

Charlie could still remember when Walter had first brought him into the casinos. Charlie had been fifteen—too young to cross the red ropes, but old enough to understand what Walter had been talking about when he spotted the hungry greed in people's eyes. The message had gone through loud and clear, and Charlie had never gambled a penny he wouldn't be happy to lose.

Did Angela's son—the paperwork named him Tony—have a Walter in his life? Someone to teach him right from wrong? A man who taught him what it meant to be a man? Charlie hoped so, but if Angela was looking to him for that, she was setting herself up for disappointment.

A high school dropout and a man the media made out to be a womanizer, Charlie would be a pathetic excuse for a role model. Hell, he'd managed to make a nice career for himself through the less-than-respectable path of professional poker, but even that was fading.

Charlie turned at a tap on his shoulder. A svelte blonde smiled down at him. "This seat taken?"

"Not that I know of."

She sat and scooted her chair toward Charlie so the outside of their legs touched. "You don't mind me taking your money, do you?"

"It's a personal code of mine to only lose to the most beautiful women," Charlie admitted.

"So, you come here a lot?" she asked. She chomped a piece of gum and winked at the dealer as he passed out their cards.

Charlie tossed a glance to the stage, where two exotic dancers did a little bump and grind against each other. "No," he admitted. "This is my first time."

"The Black Diamond isn't just a strip club, ya know."

Charlie raised a brow.

"It's some of the best damn poker in Vegas. These guys"—she gestured to the men around the table—"some of the best amateurs around."

"Hear, hear!" a man barked from the other side of the table.

"So you're a regular?"

The smile dropped from the woman's face. The man next to her tipped his cowboy hat to cover his features, but it didn't cover his chuckle.

"Do you know the guy who runs this place?" Charlie asked her.

Another chuckle from the cowboy. Charlie spared him a glance but returned his attention to the woman.

"You could say that." She turned her attention to her cards, indicating the conversation was over.

"When could I find him here, do you think?"

"Why? Spencer owe you money?" the cowboy asked.

"Not exactly," Charlie said cautiously.

"He sleep with your girlfriend?" the guy across the table offered.

Charlie lowered his voice so only the blonde could hear. "Sounds like he doesn't have the best reputation," he murmured.

"Don't believe everything these hacks tell you," she said softly.

Charlie nodded, understanding when to push and when to pull back. It was a skill that came from years of razzing guys at the poker table.

Charlie finished the hand, then folded the next early. He slipped a few chips to the dealer before standing. He'd only just turned away when the blonde grabbed him.

Charlie dropped his gaze to where her long, manicured fingers had shackled his wrist. Her bare arms were thin and bronzed. He knew her type—looking for a sugar daddy at a poker table. He didn't have the heart to tell her she was going about it all wrong. The men here didn't want to take care of her. They wanted to screw her and go home. There was a time he would have wanted to as well. "Can I help you?" he asked.

She dropped her chin and looked up at him so she was looking through her lashes. "I know who you are," she whispered. "You were pulling your punches with this bunch, weren't you?"

"That's a flattering assumption." He gave her the signature Charlie "the Devil" Singleton smile. He could take her back to his suite, but why bother? She'd just want him to play the part of the womanizing bad boy when he'd much rather be himself. The idea of how the night would play out bored him, had him as weary as a dull, thudding headache. "Good night."

He headed up toward the exit, not bothering to cash in his chips. He'd use the same pile tomorrow.

As he worked his way through the crowd toward the exit, he tossed a final glance over his shoulder. On the stage, a woman wearing a black thong and pasties wrapped her body around a pole. Men from the edges of the stage reached their hands in her direction, greedy for the opportunity to tuck a bill in her g-string.

Charlie took a cab back to his hotel, where he was flexing his bank account for two weeks in a high-roller penthouse suite. Charlie would have as soon stayed in one of Grand Escape's basic rooms, but his agent had insisted that part of Charlie's image control must be continuing to live as he had before. Sponsors didn't want to put their name on some washed-up, old-news player, so Charlie had to do everything in his power to maintain the image of the carefree bad boy he'd been for so many years.

When he arrived at the hotel, Charlie handed the driver his fare and a generous tip. He nodded to the doorman and winked at the girl behind the front desk. Everyone at Grand Escape knew him and treated him like a VIP, and he did his best never to let on how uncomfortable that made him. He hadn't gotten into poker to get rich; he'd started playing because it was the only thing he was good at.

Charlie used his room card to get the elevator to his floor. When he got to his suite, he pulled out his laptop and opened the video of one of his competitors at his last tournament. The guy was a wiz with the cards, and Charlie had yet to discover any tells. He didn't even fidget.

But when the video came on the screen, Charlie couldn't focus. His mind kept drifting back to the possibility of being a father. Charlie had wasted too many years filled with bitterness toward a father he'd never known. Had his child felt the same way? Was the kid even his?

He'd never had unprotected sex. His mother had taught him right. But even diligent use of condoms didn't guarantee a thing.

He ran a hand through his hair and closed his eyes. He didn't want to think about this anymore. Until he had answers, thinking about it was just a mind-fuck. He needed to think about something else.

His mind instantly landed on Riley. There was something he didn't want to get out of his mind. Not her or that fucking sexy get-up he'd bought her. He imagined her dark hair swishing against the pale skin of her back as he helped her lace up the leather corset. He just wanted to sit in a room and watch her walk around in snug leather, her breasts pressed high, her ass exposed in the thong.

What kind of idiot man wouldn't want Riley to wear that for him? It wasn't that Charlie didn't love nude—hell, it was his healthy respect for nude that made him appreciate lingerie so much. Lingerie teased, hinted at nude. Made a promise like the tip of a female tongue against cock before she took him in her mouth.

He'd been somehow gratified to learn that she had a whole collection of the naughty stuff, as if someone had confirmed every private image he'd ever had of her.

He closed his eyes and groaned. He was rock hard again. Thoughts of Riley did that to him.

How serious could she be about a guy she couldn't wear lingerie for?

He was ready to find out.

...

"How did your date go last night?"

Riley looked up from her keyboard to see her father standing before her, suit jacket draped over his arm. His tie was off, a sure sign he was done doing business for the day. "It was good."

Quinton nodded. "Chaz seems to be a nice boy."

Riley laughed. "He's thirty-two—hardly a boy, Daddy."

"You're all kids to me." He ran a hand threw his thinning

gray hair. He'd been doing that a lot lately. Riley's heart squeezed, knowing he was so uncomfortable with aging. Much like Sean Connery and Harrison Ford, her father had aged well, and didn't look anywhere near his true seventy-four years. "Do you have plans tonight?"

"I have to finish up a few things here and then I have dance class but no other plans."

Her father frowned. Though he tried not to say much about it, he hated her decision to continue dancing. He worried.

"Daddy, relax. It's just what I do for exercise." She reached across her desk and squeezed his hand. "I'm not her," she said in a whisper.

He nodded. "I know that." His voice was gruff. If the rest of the business world knew what a softie this hotelier was under his hardnosed exterior, it might be the death of his empire. "Do you need any money…for anything?"

Riley smiled and shook her head. "I have everything I need." He'd never be comfortable with her insistence that she make her own way, but she had to credit him for never pushing too hard.

She wasn't privy to what had gone on behind the scenes when her father had taken custody of her thirteen years ago, but her mother hadn't even been in the ground before Riley had been swept off to Quinton Carter's mansion, a tiny pink suitcase containing her favorite things in her hand. She'd been shown around her new home and told she wouldn't want for anything anymore. When Quinton had come home from work that night, he'd found her in her new room—a space decked out in pink and ballerinas just for her. She'd been sitting on the edge of the bed, terrified to touch anything. It was all too new. Too beautiful. Too intimidating for a girl who'd grown up with so little.

She'd trembled at the sight of him. He was such a massive man with a booming voice and a reputation for a cold heart. Her mother was gone, and he was all she had. Would he kick her out if he realized she'd killed her mother? Did he know her mother would still be alive if she hadn't been a spoiled brat who insisted on new ballet slippers?

Overcome with grief and guilt, the words "I'm sorry" had slipped from her lips. She hadn't meant to say them out loud.

Her father had dropped to his knees in front of her, wrapped his big arms around her tiny frame, and cried. She'd stiffened at first, unsure what to do, but then it felt so good to have someone hold her that she cried too.

It was the only time in her life she'd ever seen her father cry. They'd never talked about it, but those tears had formed a bond between father and daughter—a bond they'd desperately needed to begin their new life together. She didn't know what her life with the strange man would be like, but when she learned he'd already lost one daughter, she'd vowed not to disappoint him. All through her teens and early twenties, she had broken her vow only once, and it had gotten her sent away.

"I'll see you in the morning," she said, smiling at him.

"Have a nice dance class, Riley."

As Riley watched her father walk out the door, her phone buzzed.

The screen read: *Message from Charles Spencer.*

She bit her lip. *Chaz.* Their date hadn't ended so well last night, and she wasn't sure if he really would text like he promised. She hit *OK.*

I can't stop thinking about yesterday.

Riley put her fingers to her lips but couldn't stop them from spreading into a grin. She took a breath. *You've been on my mind, too,* she typed. Did it sound too needy? Too desperate? She wanted to improve her sex life with Chaz more than a dieter wanted ice cream, but she wasn't sure how to go about it. She held her breath and hit *Send.*

She stared at the phone, willing it to vibrate, willing him to respond.

Nothing.

"Don't be stupid, Riley. You don't need to text back and forth like teenagers all day. He's busy. Get back to work." She stole a last glance at her phone and turned back to her computer.

It buzzed again, vibrating against the desk. She chewed on her bottom lip. She should *not* be this excited about a text message.

But she was. She snatched her phone and read the message.

Did you try it on?

Her heart kicked up a beat. Surely he didn't mean…*Try what on?* she typed. *Send.*

Black. Leather. Sexy as fuck? Ring any bells?

She shifted in her chair. Was this a side of Chaz she hadn't seen? Was he secretly someone her ING would come out and purr for? That would be a good thing, right? Why did that seem so weird to her?

Her stomach clenched. All she could do was find out. *I tried it on.*

Four words. Safe. Noncommittal. He wouldn't run screaming in the other direction. And if he didn't like the idea of her wearing something so provocative…*Sexy as fuck.* She shifted again. He liked it. She hit *Send* and her lame-o message fled from her phone.

She waited, listening to the wall clock *tick, tick, tick*…Her phone buzzed.

I wish I'd been there. Hope you took pictures.

She frowned. Okay, she didn't expect that from Chaz.

Pretend it's Charlie, her ING said. *What's weird from Chaz is hot from Charlie.*

That was a terrible idea, of course, to think about Charlie while Chaz was texting her. But she reread the message and imagined Charlie typing it, that cocky grin on his face, his dimple making an occasional appearance—

Her thighs flexed instinctively. She looked around her empty office, her skin heating. She was turned on at work, one wall between her and the room where her father made billion-dollar business transactions. Dear God. She ran her tongue over her bottom lip and stared at the message, her pulse hammering. What should she say? Did he want her to be suggestive? She wasn't sure she knew how…

What would you say if you were having this conversation with Charlie?

I wish you had been too, she typed. Not exactly Anais Nin, but it was something. She hit *Send* before she could talk herself out of it, then she said a little prayer that her life was about to get a little more interesting.

She gripped the phone in her hands, staring at the display. *Tick, tick, tick.*

...

CHARLIE SINGLETON had woken up with a hard-on that far exceeded his average morning wood, and it was all thanks to little Miss Riley Carter and that black leather sexpot outfit.

He reread her last text. *I wish you had been too.*

Jesus. He hadn't expected that. He'd picked up his phone and sent her a text to tease her. She'd startled the hell out of him when she said she'd been thinking about him…and now she wished he had been there when she'd tried on the bustier? God help him.

Did you think about anyone when you put it on? he typed, ignoring that his cock jumped at the idea, demanding his attention. He wasn't about to cut this conversation short just to stroke one out.

Her reply came quickly.

I did.

He grinned. And wasn't that why he'd bought the damn thing for her—so she'd *have* to think about him? Riley was too much of a good girl for her own good, and for some reason the idea of making her break that mold had fascinated him since the day Lacey had introduced them.

He settled back onto his pillows and looked at the ceiling. She worked in this very building, in one of the many offices in the tower over the casino. She tried to blend in with the stuffed shirts and the blowhards like she was one of them, when he knew she was really much more underneath. Why did the idea of making her hot and bothered while she was alone in her office turn him on so much?

Ah, but that was why they called him the Devil.

How did it look? Are you happy with it, or do I need to take you shopping for a different one?

He hadn't expected any of this when he picked up his phone to push her buttons. And now he'd pay. His cock was fucking granite, threatening to bust out of his boxers.

He set his phone on his chest, closed his eyes, and imagined her in her office chair, cheeks tinged with that perpetual flush she had in his presence, as if his mere existence were scandalous. She probably had her dark hair pulled back in a clip like she preferred to wear it for work, and was wearing one of those business suits that weren't supposed to be sexy but were on her because of the way they pulled a little across her ass.

His phone beeped, alerting him to a new text, and he smiled. Looked like Riley wanted to play.

I'm happy with it. You liked it, then?

He thought he'd made that pretty damn clear yesterday. *I liked it, but I have no doubt I'd like it more on you.*

Was this the text after which she'd finally say he'd taken it too far? He thought about adding more but left it at that, unwilling to scare her away if he could avoid it. He punched *Send*.

Her response came quickly—as if she'd been typing it before he'd sent the last message. *I've never worn leather panties before.*

He closed his eyes. Her ass would look so sweet in that red leather thong. And if she wore it for him, he'd roll her on her stomach, kiss his way down her back, touching his tongue to all the exposed pieces of flesh between the leather lacings. When he reached her ass, he'd graze his teeth over the firm flesh of each cheek before sliding his hand underneath her to cup her mound, rocking his palm against her so her swollen clit rubbed against the leather there.

His fantasy was interrupted by another message coming through.

I'm sorry. I didn't mean to make you uncomfortable.

He moaned. *You're making me uncomfortable, all right, but not in the way you mean. Don't apologize. That's what they make cold showers for.*

He hit *Send* and he closed his eyes. What would she do if he went over to her office? He'd indulged in that particular fantasy more than once while staying at this hotel. Hell, truth was, he could have stayed anywhere. In some ways, it would have been better to stay at a hotel that wasn't hosting the tournament, but he always stayed here. He'd never let himself overthink it. He just did it. Because being near Riley felt good. Because flirting with her was fun.

His phone beeped.

Good. I mean, I'm kind of uncomfortable in that way too.

Groaning, he adjusted his dick. Maybe he'd always stayed here because he believed something like this could happen. He would go into her office without warning, lock the door behind him, and push her up against the wall…

Hell, he couldn't fuck her in her office when she had a boyfriend any more than he could go all in holding an unsuited seven and two. But he could text with the best of them.

You know what would look good with that get-up? he typed.

Her response came back quickly. *Tell me.*

Leather handcuffs.

If that didn't scare her off, then, well, maybe he *would* go up there.

You're into that?

He raised a brow. Really, as depraved as she seemed to think he was, the question took him by surprise. *I can be into a lot of things if the mood is right and both parties are willing.*

You'll have to show me sometime.

That had him shooting up in bed. Holy shit.

What exactly had happened on that date of hers last night? Had she finally seen her boyfriend for the tool he was? Would that be enough to have good girl Riley honest to God suggesting he tie her up sometime?

He frowned…or maybe someone else had her phone. He scowled at his display. Hadn't she said she'd lost her cell? Had she ever found it? Had Lacey found it?

If Lacey was fucking with him, he was going to kill her.

He climbed out of bed and tugged on his jeans, exercising great caution as he zipped them. He'd go to Riley's office, find out she'd lost her phone or forgotten it somewhere, and stop looking like a complete fool to whoever was on the other end of this conversation.

He grabbed the first t-shirt he saw in his suitcase. He pulled it over his head as he strode out of his suite. He was at the elevator when his phone beeped.

I'm kidding, of course.

That confused him even more. If Lacey was screwing with him, why would she pull back like that? If it was Lacey, she was trying really damn hard to be convincing.

Grand Escape was set up with two towers. The casino sprawled across the first floor, and there was a tower for the guest rooms and a tower for Carter Hotels and Entertainment executive offices. He had to go down to the first floor to get to the business offices, and by the time he was on the second elevator his phone was beeping again.

Okay, I feel really stupid now.

Damn. He let out a breath. But what if it was her? If Riley was coming out of her shell, he didn't want to throw up walls. He wanted to throw down the red carpet.

The elevator opened to her floor and he typed a message as he walked toward her office.

Don't. He sent the single-word reply.

There.

He didn't knock on her door when he reached her office. Instead, he barged in and was greeted with the image of her sitting behind her desk. Her hair was pinned back at her neck, but one little strand had escaped and was beginning to curl. Her cheeks were flushed, and she chewed on her bottom lip as she stared at her cell phone.

"Riley?"

Her head snapped up and her eyes grew wide. "Charlie? What are you doing here?"

He wouldn't have thought it was possible, but the pink in her cheeks deepened. "I—" Hell. What could he say? He wanted to see her let loose a little. Calling her out as soon as she started to let go was hardly going to help. He smiled. "Can I take you to breakfast?"

She laughed. "It's almost four in the afternoon."

Shit. Right. Suits like her had been up for hours now. "Right. Lunch then?"

"I already ate. Four hours ago." She wrinkled her nose, and he thought, *So damn sweet*. "What's this about?"

"It's—" He looked at her phone. Okay, so she didn't want to talk about it. "I just want to take you to lunch…or dinner, or whatever."

Her eyes drifted down his body and to his crotch, where his jeans were fitting a little tighter than they should, thanks to their texts.

He grinned. "Let me take you out, Riley. I need to get away from the usual suspects."

She stood in a fluid motion of grace and long limbs. "I have dance in half an hour." She slung her purse over one shoulder and clutched her phone in her hand.

"Let me walk you out," he said.

She nodded, smiling at him as he held the door for her. "Are you enjoying your stay at Grand Escape?"

He watched her hips sway as she led the way down the hall. She had one of those bodies with a tiny waist and splayed hips. The kind that made a man want to run his hands from waist to hip and test the breadth.

He was imagining those bare hips flaring under the leather corset when she tossed a glance over her shoulder. "Has there been a problem?"

"No." He caught up with her in three long strides. "Your hotel is lovely, as always."

He slowed when they got to the elevators, but she kept walking. "Ry?"

"What?" She stopped and he motioned to the elevator. "Oh, no. No. I'm…" She shook her head. "I take the stairs. It's good exercise."

He narrowed his gaze. "You walk down twenty-two flights of stairs every day? For the exercise?"

"And up," she said softly. "It's not a big deal."

That did a lot to explain her fantastic ass. "Treat yourself today," he said. "Come on. Live dangerously."

She turned, but he saw her swallow hard before her face was out of his line of sight. "I'll pass," she said before slipping into the stairwell.

Charlie smelled bullshit and followed her. "Why don't you just put your office on the first floor?" he asked when he'd caught up with her.

"Because my father likes the office with the best view, so I'd have to walk up for meetings all day long anyway."

Charlie smirked. Right. She did it for exercise. "Are you afraid of elevators, Riley?"

She stopped on the landing and looked at her feet. "Not afraid, exactly. I choose not to use them."

He tipped her chin up and ran his thumb along her jaw. "Why?"

Her eyes dropped to his lips. "Why what?"

What had he been saying? He had no idea. Because those green eyes were on his mouth and all his blood had left his brain and headed south.

She shook her head, breaking the thick tension between them, and looked at her phone again. What? Did she think he was going to send her a text when he was standing right here? He wasn't above it, if that's what it took.

"Come out with me tonight. I'll pick you up after your dance class. I want to talk to you about"—he scrambled for a good excuse—"an idea I had for Lacey's birthday."

She frowned. Maybe she was afraid he was going to hold her to her little suggestion about the handcuffs.

He held up both hands. "Completely platonic. I promise I won't come on to you." Then, because he couldn't help himself, he added, "Unless you want me to."

A small smile curved her pink lips and he bit back a groan, thinking of how badly he wanted to put that smile in a whole new context. "Okay," she said softly, turning to continue their long journey down the stairs. "For Lacey. But you have to be on your best behavior."

"You have my word," he said. And he meant it. Mostly.

CHAPTER
FOUR

Riley grabbed her water bottle and tried to catch her breath. Dance class had been brutal tonight. Around her the other dancers were bent at the waist, trying to pull precious oxygen into their lungs.

This was what Riley loved about dance. Jazz. Modern. Ballet. Ballroom. She loved it all. It was hard. Pounding. Demanding. A brutal reminder of what her body could do when she pushed it to its limits. It made her feel alive.

Alysse, her instructor, crossed the room and threw a towel to Riley. "You were *on* tonight, girl."

Riley grabbed her towel and wiped the sweat from her forehead. Alysse taught what was quickly becoming Riley's favorite class: a mashup of jazz, hip-hop, and ballet that tested limits. "Thanks. I found my groove, I think."

Alysse grinned and flashed a glance over her shoulder before lowering her voice. "Listen, my dance company is having auditions next week. I'd like to see you there."

Riley waved away the suggestion. "Whatever, we both know I'm not the caliber dancer to go pro." The invitation made her smile, though. Sometimes, as she danced, she imagined she could one day be the kind of dancer her mother had been…before the drugs.

Alysse raised her brow. "Yes, you are. You're the real thing, Riley."

Riley frowned. "You're serious."

"As a heart attack."

"I'm almost twenty-six," she said, because that was middle-aged in dancer years.

"All the more reason not to wait." Alysse gave a small shrug. "Listen, I'm not about the hard sell. There are plenty of beautiful dancers out there who would be great fit. It's an opportunity I wanted you to know about. A week from Saturday, five p.m., here in the studio. What you do with that information is up to you."

Riley nodded. "Okay. Thanks," she said, but she knew she wouldn't audition. She did, though, for a moment, indulge in the fantasy of being just another girl in her twenties being given the opportunity to dance. She envied them.

Her phone beeped, and she dug in her bag to get it. *Message from Charles Spencer.* She smiled. She wasn't sure what had changed, but Chaz was thinking about her a lot right now. Good. Maybe this was just the change they needed.

She opened her phone and read the message.

Don't be mad, but I came by the studio and watched you dance.

Her breath caught in her throat. He'd watched her? He'd never expressed an interest in her dancing before, and she'd thought he didn't care. In fact, it always seemed like he was trying to get her to skip dance class to do something with him, and she'd wondered if her father hadn't told him how much he disapproved of the activity.

The phone beeped again.

I've never seen anything as beautiful as the way you move. Or as sexy.

She pulled her lower lip into her mouth. He couldn't possibly know what that meant to her. *Thank you.*

You should be on stage. Your dance is an art, meant to be shared.

Something in the pit of her stomach warmed, and the sensation radiated through her. Maybe there was more to Chaz than she'd realized. *We both know how my father would feel about that*, she typed. *Besides, a career in dance isn't very profitable but for the select few.* She added the last because she knew Chaz was practical, and she didn't want him thinking she was hung up on her father's approval.

Who cares what your father thinks? You're amazing, and if he's got half a brain he'll support you in whatever you do.

Riley blinked. Who was this man, and what had he done with the guy she'd been dating for two years?

And why did the change make her so happy?

...

CHARLIE WINKED at the hostess as he strode into the Black Diamond. He'd decided to check out the club and see what he could learn about its manager. Whether he was this invested in digging up dirt on Chaz or it was a convenient excuse to escape the images turning through his mind, he wasn't sure. Riley in black Lycra dance clothes. Riley moving and bending her beautiful body to music he couldn't hear but could practically *feel* just by watching her slide through the room. Riley looking like the most beautiful thing he'd ever seen.

He wasn't sure what had inspired him to swing by her dance studio, but it had left him questioning what the hell he thought he was doing by taking her to dinner. Like it or not, she was another man's woman.

His phone buzzed at his side, and he snatched it, hoping it was Riley.

Good thing he knew how to handle disappointment.

"Rick, how you doing, man?"

"Singleton, I've been trying to get a hold of you all day."

"Yeah, well, there was a girl. I figured you'd catch me later. Turns out I was right."

"With you, there's always a girl." His agent chuckled. "Listen, I wish I had better news."

Charlie winced. This was why he'd been avoiding his agent's call. "Out with it." His eyes wandered to a dark-haired man at the stage. The dick grabbed a dancer by her long blond hair and pulled her to him, his face fierce. Where the hell was the bouncer?

Rick rambled on about endorsement deals and sponsorships, money and payouts—all the shit Charlie hated about being in professional poker and all the reasons he gave Rick fifteen percent of his money.

Watching the man stick his finger in the dancer's face, Charlie clenched his fist. He didn't care if a woman was a stripper or the queen of England; she deserved to be treated with respect.

"The fact of the matter is," Rick was saying, "if you want a poker website to sponsor you for this tournament, you're gonna have to shake up your image. UltimatePokerPowerhouse.net is interested, but they've hinted that they're worried about the amount of camera time you're going to get. They said unless you can guarantee a win—"

"Rick, you know this game changed when all the internet poker amateurs started buying in to the big tourneys. With guys playing fast and loose, it's anyone's game." A fact that frustrated the old-timers. Charlie hadn't cared...until sponsors started dropping him.

Professional players made most of their money through sponsorships, and sponsors wanted the camera on their logo as often as possible. Players could get that screen time by being a consistent winner or by bringing outside interests to the table— scandal, sensation, anything the viewers would eat up.

"You know, what you need," Rick went on, "is another Nicole Abucee. Then we'd land any sponsorship we wanted."

Nicole was the Hollywood starlet who had left her producer/director husband and come to Charlie's house the same night. At the time, Charlie had wanted to strangle the pap member who had snuck into his backyard and taken pictures of them in Charlie's hot tub. In retrospect, he was pretty sure Nicole had tipped them off.

"Seems cheap, Rick."

As Charlie let Rick drone on about other long-shot deals, a waitress wearing pasties and a smile approached Charlie. "A drink?"

Charlie covered his phone with his hand and nodded to the stage where the man had been manhandling the stripper. "Where's your bouncer? That asshat needs thrown out of here."

Her frown creased her heavy makeup. "That's Chaz Spencer. He runs this place, or—let me tell you—I'd kick his ass out myself." She sighed. "Anyway, that's his girl. She brings it on herself by messing around with him."

Charlie narrowed his eyes at the man who was now sitting back and enjoying a lap dance from the blonde. Riley could do a fuck of a lot better than that. "Thanks for the info," he muttered. "I don't need a drink." He slid the waitress a twenty, and she grinned.

Charlie returned his attention to the phone as Rick asked, "Do you want to keep playing poker or not, Singleton?"

"Of course." But it wasn't so much a *want* as a *have no other options*. What else could he do? He had no skills, no formal education beyond the tenth grade. Poker was his life.

He narrowed his eyes at Chaz again. "Listen, tip off those reporter friends of yours that Riley Carter and I will be at the Eiffel Tower restaurant tonight."

"Riley Carter? Las Vegas' Good Daughter?"

"That's right." Maybe a couple of pictures in the papers would help them both out. The publicity would help Charlie get his sponsorship and maybe, just maybe, it would help Riley out of a relationship with Manhandling, Cheating Dick over there.

"Consider it done. But do me a favor, Singleton?"

"What?"

"Make it good."

...

"OH MY God," Lacey said from the couch. "Did you see this? Paris Hilton has a new beau."

Riley rolled her eyes and dropped her gym bag by the door. "My day was fine, Lace. How was yours?" She didn't have to look to know that Lacey was watching G! TV—Today's Gossip about Tomorrow's Celebrities! The channel was something of an addiction for Lacey.

Lacey snickered, shrugging. "Sorry. I just think it's interesting, trying to imagine a life with that kind of money, that kind of luxury." Her brow pinched. "To be honest, I'm not sure how you pass it up. I mean, who wants to work every day?"

Riley frowned. "Why would I want a life that would make me a joke in the eyes of the media?" At eighteen Riley had set out to prove herself to a world that assumed she was just another spoiled little rich girl. Although she knew her father would like to see her work a little less and enjoy life a little more, she liked to think he was proud of the life she'd built on her own.

Lacey shifted on the couch and pulled her legs under her. "Why do you assume you would have been a bad egg? Lots of people have money and don't make a fool of themselves."

Riley shrugged. "Who knows? Maybe I have a little bit of a wild side, and a little too much indulgence would make it come out in full force."

Lacey laughed. "Wild? Sure, Ry. Whatever you say."

She plopped on the couch beside her friend, who—like nearly everyone else in the world—knew nothing about Riley's rebellious months as a sixteen-year-old...the ones immediately preceding her father's decision to send her to girls' school. "I can be wild."

"Uh-huh."

"I think if I let myself have access to all that money, my ING would just be an NG. She wouldn't be hidden and tucked away where she has to stay out of trouble. She'd be out, flaunting herself like Britney of the no-panties days." She was her mother's daughter, after all, and Cynthia Dreier had the wildest of wild sides—Riley just hadn't known until after her mother was gone.

"Maybe showing her to the world would do you some good."

Riley looked at the television where Paris was dirty dancing with some football player at an LA club. "You know, the press should give her a break. Paris isn't the only ditzy blonde who likes to have a little fun from time to time."

"Of course she's not." Lacey smirked, studying the TV. "But she sure is entertaining."

"The only reason it's an issue is because of who her grandfather is." Riley smiled as Jaws jumped up on the couch with her. "So, no, I'm not jealous of Paris. I'm jealous of girls who *don't* have a potential multimillion-dollar inheritance. Because they can be whoever they want to be without having cameras trained on them."

"I'm pretty sure you can indulge in a little luxury without making a sex tape."

Jaws licked Riley's face, and she grinned. "I already have a sex tape."

Lacey punched Riley's arm. "Get out!"

Riley winced, rubbing her triceps. "Sure, just last Christmas I caught Jaws on tape humping Santa's leg at the company Christmas party."

Lacey gave a dramatic eye roll. "Right. Well, girl, if that's the most scandalous thing you have going on in your life, I suggest to kick it up a notch."

"Wouldn't that be nice," Riley said with a sigh.

Furrowing her brow, Lacey grabbed the remote and clicked off the T.V. She turned on the couch so she was facing Riley. "But you can still be a *little* scandalous in private. People aren't watching you all the time."

No, thanks to years of good behavior, it was rare to find paparazzi following her these days. Sure, there was the occasional story about how simply she lived or how hard she worked, facts that had her dubbed early on as "Vegas' Good Daughter," but those stories only sold papers if they were accompanied by fall-from-grace stories. As long as she was boring, they'd leave her alone.

She stood, pulling out her hair tie. She only had thirty minutes before Charlie Singleton would be here. "I'm going to jump in the shower," she told her roommate as she stood.

Lacey raised a brow, watching Riley over the back of the couch. "Another date with Chaz?"

A smile curved Riley's lips at the mention of her boyfriend's name. Lacey might not be Team Chaz now, but if Riley told her about the text messages he'd started sending her, maybe she'd see the light. "Not tonight," she answered. The talk about the latest developments in her relationship with Chaz would have to wait for another time. "Your brother's taking me out tonight." *That* also made her smile. Dear God, she was a mess. Thoughts of spending an evening with Charlie shouldn't make her giddy.

Lacey pushed herself to her knees and propped her elbows on the back of the couch. "My brother? Maybe you *are* being a little scandalous in private, and you're just not telling me about it."

Riley bit her lip as she remembered why she'd agreed to dinner with Charlie. She couldn't tell Lacey he wanted to talk about her birthday—Charlie might be planning a surprise. Instead she just shrugged. "He promised to keep it platonic."

Lacey snorted. "Have you *met* my brother?"

CHAPTER
FIVE

"You've got to be kidding me," Riley said when their cab pulled up outside the Eiffel Tower replica. She turned to Charlie. "You know I can't do this, right?"

He opened the door and stepped out. Reaching back in for her hand, he said, "I know no such thing."

He ducked under the doorframe and smiled. His grin, charming and wide and just for her, made her stomach flip-flop.

"You need a ride somewhere, miss?" the cabby asked.

She shook her head. She wouldn't make a fool of Charlie over some ridiculous fear. With a deep breath, she put her hand in his and slid out of the cab.

As the taxi pulled away, Charlie squeezed her hand, and she raised her eyes to the top of the tower.

That was a mistake.

"I think I'm going to be sick," she whispered, swallowing the ball of panic in her throat. It wasn't the height that did it. Not exactly. It was knowing how she'd have to get there.

"Hey, look at me." Charlie tilted her chin up with his thumb.

She blinked. They locked eyes. He kept her hand enclosed in his.

"Now, close your eyes."

She did as he said, because the alternative was looking over his shoulder and thinking about being trapped in the elevator that would take them to the dining area. "I can't do it, Charlie," she said softly.

"Keep your eyes closed," he said. "Think about something else."

She swallowed. Her hand felt small in his big one. His skin was hot on hers. "Like what?"

His next word came as a hot whisper against her ear: "Sex."

Her eyes flew open. "Charlie, you promised."

"Do you trust me?"

The reasonable answer to that question was *no*, but she found herself nodding. Against all her better judgment, she'd always trusted Charlie "the Devil" Singleton. She thought that was why they'd given him that moniker in poker—he was so smooth, so damn charming, you trusted him even when you knew trusting him would cost you.

When Charlie was around, she could count on three things: making a fool of herself and him laughing it off like it didn't matter, going gooey inside every time he smiled, and trusting him against her better judgment.

Looking into his eyes now, she felt the last two in full effect and wondered when she could expect the first to arrive. Probably soon, if she had to get in an elevator. "I don't want to go up there. Let's go somewhere else." She had to gulp in air as she imagined it. She couldn't get in that elevator. She liked being able to see more than two feet in any direction, preferred having the earth beneath her feet. "Do we have to?" she asked.

Charlie tilted her chin up. "You're tough, and I know you can do this. I picked it because it's a glass elevator, so if it's claustrophobia that gets to you…" He studied her face. "We can leave right now if you want to."

Her insides warmed and relaxed a bit. "You mean that, don't you?"

"Of course I do."

She shook her head. "I don't want to be afraid."

He smiled and squeezed her fingers in his. "You're tougher than you think, sweetheart."

"Yeah, right."

"It's true. Now close those gorgeous green eyes again."

She obeyed, followed him two steps, and stalled.

She knew he'd closed the space between them because she could feel the heat of his body, could feel his breath against her cheek. "You're thinking again, Riley. You need to turn that off once in a while. Tell me, what's your favorite thing about living in Vegas?"

She frowned. He was leading her again, staying closer this time as she took small, blind steps to follow. "Who says I have a favorite thing? Maybe I hate living here."

She wanted to open her eyes at the hearty sound of his chuckle but didn't dare. If she was going to do this—if she wanted to make it to the top without a panic attack—she needed to keep her eyes closed.

"You can't fool me, Riley," he said. "There's something keeping you here or you would have left already. So, tell me, what is it you love so much about Vegas?"

"I work in the hospitality industry. Why would I move? It's like a smorgasbord of jobs for someone like me here."

She heard his *tsk-tsk* followed by a very clear *ding*. She jumped, her eyes flying open.

They were in the elevator. And it was moving. They were in a small, moving elevator. They were in a very small, moving elevator and she didn't know how long they'd been here and how much longer it would take. Had they stalled?

Charlie cleared his throat and loosened her grip on his jacket. "Not that I'm complaining about having you this close to me," he whispered, his breath hot against her ear. "In fact, I could get used to it."

She was glued to him, she realized vaguely, but she couldn't contemplate moving. Not until those doors opened.

"It's just, Riley, baby, if you're going to have your body this close to mine, I want you to be looking desperately at *me*, not a pair of elevator doors. Do you have any idea what that does to a guy's ego?"

She frowned. "I'm not worried about your ego," she muttered.

"Hey." He was stroking her back, soft circles between her shoulder blades. "You're shaking."

"I prefer the stairs," she whispered.

"Close your eyes."

She shook her head, staring at the doors. Like Charlie had promised, the elevator was glass, and that relieved a little of her claustrophobia. If they got stuck, people would be able to see they were inside. They'd be okay. Someone would come help them.

The elevator's second *ding* signaled their arrival, and the doors slid open to the famous bustling kitchen of the French restaurant she'd always been curious about but never visited.

The maître d' smiled. "Reservations?"

"Singleton," Charlie said. And just like that, they were being led out of that death trap of an elevator and to their table.

When the concierge pulled out a chair for her, Riley gasped at the view. Their seats were right next to the floor-to-ceiling windows overlooking the eleven-story-high view of the fountains at the Bellagio.

"Will the heights bother you?" Charlie asked in a whisper.

She shook her head and slid into her chair, angling it strategically so she wouldn't miss a second of the vision outside the window. "It's beautiful."

The concierge placed a leather-bound menu before her. She opened it and gaped. Quick mental calculations told her a basic meal here could more than pay for her next shopping spree at Fredrick's. When she looked up, Charlie was studying her.

"You're doing it again," she said, feeling her cheeks warm.

"Doing what?" Charlie asked, eyeing her over his menu.

Flames of heat licked higher in her cheeks. She wished she was one of those women with a cute flush, but hers pinkened her whole face. She leaned forward and lowered her voice to a whisper. "You're looking at me like I'm the sprinkles on a brownie sundae."

His gaze dropped to her mouth, then the little of her body

not hidden behind the table. Though she was covered by a black, high-necked number she'd chosen for modesty, the heat in his eyes made her feel exposed. His focus shifted back to her mouth before he said, "Sweetheart, you're the whole damn sundae, and I am more than ready for dessert."

She looked around them. Had anybody heard? Did she hope they had or hadn't? "You promised you'd behave," she whispered.

He raised a brow, the picture of innocence. "You're the one who brought it up."

Their server approached their table. "The wine you requested, sir," he said, placing a bottle on the table. "May I get you started with the roasted *foie gras* tonight?"

"Please," Charlie said.

Riley chewed on her lip, calculating her budget. Everyone assumed that because her father was this big hotelier, she had a bottomless checking account, but the opposite was true. She took pride in being frugal, in stretching every dollar. In paying her own way.

"Riley," Charlie said softly.

She lifted her gaze from the menu to meet his. Damn but he was handsome. She'd always loved those blue eyes.

"Dinner's on me. Relax."

She frowned. "I can't let you do that."

His chest shook with his deep, rich chuckle. "Sure you can. I begged you to dine with me—something, I'll have you know, I don't normally do. The least I can do is pay."

"This is all pretty extravagant for a dinner to discuss Lacey's birthday."

He lifted his palms and treated her to a flash of dimple. "What can I say? My sister is *very* important to me."

"Uh-huh."

The server returned with the wine, and he and Charlie went through the ritual of sampling it before the server offered her a glass.

"Oh, no thank you. I'll have water."

The server nodded politely. "Our special is *le filet boeuf* served with a red wine sauce."

"Sounds perfect," Charlie said, closing his menu. He looked at Riley. "You too?"

Riley swallowed, lest she drool over the steak. "No, I don't eat red meat," she said. "I'll have the salmon, please."

The server took the rest of their order and excused himself.

Charlie leaned forward on his forearms. "No red meat?"

Stop smiling at me! But she couldn't very well demand that without letting him know what an effect his smile had on her and her now-gooey insides. "It's not healthy," she explained.

"Do you treat yourself to anything that isn't healthy or let yourself enjoy anything that isn't practical?"

Her cheeks burned. He knew all about her completely unpractical addiction...though he had no way of knowing what a serious addiction it was.

He chuckled. "Other than *that*. You have a practical job, wear practical clothes—with the exception of certain undergarments that are probably the healthiest thing your psyche has going for it—you eat only sensible things." He swirled his wine and took a drink. "You sure you don't want a glass of wine?"

"Thanks, but I don't drink on weeknights."

He chuckled. "See what I mean?"

She straightened. "I'm responsible."

He passed his glass to her. "No one's arguing there."

She frowned into his wine. "What do you want me to do with this?"

"Smell."

She inhaled deeply through her nose. It smelled...heavenly. Faintly flowery. She could imagine the dark red liquid rolling over her tongue. "It's nice," she said.

"Now take a sip," he said.

Frowning, she explained again, "It's a Wednesday. I don't drink on weeknights."

He nodded. "Understandable, but I'm not even asking you to have a drink. Just a taste."

His eyes burned into hers, and somehow it seemed like they

were talking about so much more than wine. *Just a taste.*

She kept her eyes locked on Charlie as she tilted the glass to her lips.

"Take a small sip, and keep it in your mouth," he said. "Let the wine slide over your tongue, over every taste bud. Experience every flavor before you swallow."

She did as he instructed and widened her eyes. The floral scent popped when she tasted it slowly like this.

"*Now*, swallow," he said softly, his gaze narrowed in on her mouth.

Something about the way he watched her made taking a single sip of wine feel like the most erotic experience of her life. Blood rushed between her legs and she squeezed them together.

She didn't want to be attracted to Charlie, but there it was. She wanted him more right now than she'd ever wanted Chaz. Even if she combined all the desire she'd ever had for Chaz, her lust in this moment outweighed it all.

She licked her lips and he exhaled slowly. Had he been holding his breath?

He swallowed, leaning back a bit. "What do you think?"

She thought she'd never enjoyed a sip of wine so much in her life. "I think it tastes…expensive."

He shook his head. "You worry too much." He lifted his glass again. "Another?"

She nodded and let him lift the glass to her lips. Because she wanted more wine or because she liked the way he looked at her as she drank, she wasn't sure. Best not to analyze it too much.

"Let's dance while we wait for our food," he said, pushing his chair out as he stood.

Riley stared at his extended hand, tempted. "I don't think that would be appropriate."

He took her left hand and ran his thumb over her bare ring finger. "I don't see why not," he said, tugging gently.

She let out a breath. She wasn't sure where things were going with her and Chaz. Truth be told, she'd been contemplating—in her weaker moments—whether or not she should end their relationship. Something had been…missing. But if this afternoon's text messages were any indication, things were about to get more interesting between them. Where was that flirtation—no, that *fire*—when they were together in person? Where had it been for the last two years?

Charlie led her to the dance floor and pulled her into his arms. At the small of her back, the heat of his hand seeped through the thin cotton of her dress. "Listen, I'm not one to complain when I have a beautiful woman in my arms, but do you want to share what's worrying you?"

She chewed on her lower lip. Maybe if she talked about Chaz the whole time, she'd feel less guilty about dancing with Charlie. "I kind of have a boyfriend, you know."

Charlie nodded politely but pulled her even closer. His words were whispered in her ear. "Any man with half a brain would make sure you were his. If you were mine, there would be no *kind of* about it."

She ignored the stirring between her legs. Damn, he was good at that. "We're taking things slowly."

"How's that going?"

Over his shoulder, she could see the now-empty wine glass sitting at their table. Hadn't she stopped drinking on weeknights because Chaz had always given her disapproving looks when she did? And here she was, drinking and dancing with another man on a Wednesday night, and she wasn't even sure if Chaz would care. "I don't really know," she finally answered. "Sometimes I think he's ready to get serious, and then he backs away. I'm not sure what he wants."

"What do *you* want?" Charlie asked against her ear.

Riley gaped. "Him, of course. He's great. We have a history. He works for my father too, so he understands the demands of my job. We make a good couple. A good fit."

Charlie made a humming sound. "Sounds…practical. What does he do for you?"

"What do you mean?" She took a shallow breath. She could hardly think when Charlie was this close.

His mouth grazed the edge of her jaw. "He doesn't like lingerie, and it's your secret joy, so I assume he makes up for it in some other way."

She licked her lips and tried to block the fingers of pleasure that began where his hand pressed against her back and radiated through her core. This man was everything she didn't need, and yet her body reacted desperately to every touch. Her ING whimpered about being thirsty and Charlie being just the refreshment she needed.

"Does he like it rough?" he asked, his voice a deep rumble against her ear. "Or maybe he ties you up? Kisses down your body, his mouth against your breasts, his tongue flicking over your nipples? Does he put his mouth between your legs and taste you, lick you until you come?"

Riley closed her eyes against the wicked pleasure betraying her between her legs. "No." Then, because that revealed too much, she said, "I mean, he's…gentle."

"Hm," he said, but the sound was filled with more condescension than understanding. "What is it about him? Do you like it slow? Thorough? Does he make you feel cherished when he's moving inside you?" He was asking about Chaz, and yet the words were whispered like foreplay.

With her body pressed against Charlie's like this, when she was so close she could feel the strength of him, could trace her fingers across the breadth of his shoulders, she couldn't imagine Charlie in a romantic relationship where sex wasn't a key ingredient. "Not all relationships revolve around sex."

He chuckled against her ear, his breath hot there. "The good ones do."

"Not all of them," she snapped, then winced at how defensive she sounded.

He stopped moving. "You *have* had sex with him, haven't you?"

She stopped moving. Only Charlie would find the possibility that they were celibate so horrifying. "We're consenting adults. We've been together."

He pulled back to study her face and raised a brow. "Sounds…

thrilling."

"You don't know everything, Charlie Singleton."

"Agreed. That's why I'm trying to find out." He studied her for a beat, then lowered his voice, his face serious for once. "He at least gets you off, doesn't he?"

Her breath caught and her cheeks heated. "That's none of your business."

"Jesus. That's a no."

"I can't believe we're having this conversation. I can't believe I'm still here with you. What exactly did you need to talk to me about, anyway?"

He pulled her close again and said, "Hey, I'm just trying to help. You looked stressed, and now I understand why."

One of his hands worked at the tension in her shoulders even as they danced. The contact or the wine turned her legs to jelly, and she let herself relax, let him work out the tension, let herself enjoy the warmth of his touch.

"Does he know about your ING?"

She froze. "I need to kill Lacey, don't I?"

He chuckled and dropped his hand down to squeeze hers. "Our food's here."

She followed him back to the table, wondering why she wasn't more insulted, why his questions didn't make her feel violated. But they didn't. In fact, considering Chaz was the man she had until very recently assumed she'd marry, they were perfectly reasonable questions.

Right, and the way he asked them made her hot. There was that too.

But this afternoon, when she and Chaz had been texting, it had been different. She and Chaz had been together, sure, but it had never been playful like that. He'd never been one for much foreplay of any kind, let alone verbal foreplay, so it gave her hope. Chaz may not know about her ING, but in the years ahead of them, their sexual relationship was bound to grow.

She sighed as she sat. Her salmon looked delicious, but tonight the forbidden steak was calling to her. Charlie caught her licking her lips and focused his gaze on her mouth. The heat in his eyes was so intense, she thought she might combust.

"Here." He tore his gaze from her mouth and cut a piece of the tender filet. "Try a bite."

Her mouth watered. Her nipples hardened under her dress. Suddenly she was sure this wasn't about food at all, but, mesmerized, she leaned forward.

"Open your mouth," he said softly, bringing the steak to her lips.

She parted her lips and let him slide the fork into her mouth. She closed her lips around the tines as the first burst of flavor hit her tongue. She let her eyes float closed as she chewed the tender beef—this decadent treat she had denied herself for years. A soft moan escaped her lips.

When she swallowed, she opened her eyes to see Charlie staring at her mouth. His lips were softly parted and his pulse thrummed at his neck. He looked like a starved man. A starved man not the least bit interested in the steak in front of him. She licked her lips. "It's good," she said lamely.

The corner of his mouth lifted in a crooked grin. He cut another bite of steak and held out his fork. "Just let go. Enjoy yourself."

Riley was so absorbed in the moment, she didn't even hear the click of the paparazzo's camera.

CHAPTER
SIX

Chaz had a plan for the man in front of him. More, he had a plan for his money. "Thanks for meeting with me, Mr. Carter."

"Call me Quinton, son," Quinton Carter said, settling into his seat with his scotch.

Chaz eyed the man whose empire he'd salivated over for the last four years. Quinton hadn't had shit when he'd been Chaz's age—nothing but cunning and drive. He'd married into his first hotel, had gotten lucky when the wench had croaked young, and had gone on to change a single hotel into the behemoth company Carter Hotels and Entertainment. Now Chaz wanted it for himself and he was so close he could almost taste it.

He took a breath. "Quinton, I'm here because I want to discuss my intentions."

"Intentions?"

"For your daughter. I've been...I hoped I could get your blessing."

Quinton put down his scotch and studied Chaz over his folded hands. "What kind of life can you give her?"

Chaz had to play this carefully. If he pushed too much, he'd get nothing, but if he didn't push at all, he might still get nothing.

"We love each other," he said, because that was where he figured he should start. "And we're both hard workers."

"You intend to remain a dual-income household?"

God bless the man's old-fashioned sensibilities. They played right into the palm of Chaz's hands. "I'd be lying if I said I wasn't hoping for the GM position. I've been looking to move up...so she won't have to work." He paused for a moment, doing his best to look unassuming.

"I'm sure you'll advance in your career, driven as you are." Quinton swirled the amber liquid in his glass. "So, you want the GM position?"

Chaz gave a soft smile. "Not as much as I want your daughter." That was his money line. He'd been waiting years to have this conversation, biding his time before delivering the perfect line at a carefully calculated moment. It was true, too. Riley had a hot bod, even if she was a bit stuffy. Eventually, Chaz would want children, and she'd make a great mother. But what made him salivate when he looked at Riley Carter was that she was the heir apparent to Quinton Carter's empire. And that was where his mild affection for Riley sprouted wings and became downright admiration.

Quinton narrowed his eyes, rubbing his beard. "She seems to be fond of you as well."

The man didn't have to seem so unhappy about it. Shifting in his seat, Chaz reached for his own scotch.

"I'm not young anymore, Spencer, and I don't have much patience for bullshit."

Chaz straightened. "Excuse me, sir?"

"I don't pretend to know your feelings for my daughter, but you're enough like I was at your age that I do know your feelings for my business."

"I am ambitious. It's true, but that is independent of my feelings for Riley."

Quinton narrowed his eyes. "And you're here because you're planning on marrying my daughter? Not because you thought you'd achieve some end by having this conversation *tonight*, two days before I announce the new position."

Chaz swallowed. This had to be a trap. "I only want your blessing to marry Riley."

"Where's the ring?"

Several dancers came through the doors, talking loudly as they came off their break.

Quinton shook his head as he watched them. "God, I loathe this place," he muttered.

Chaz winced. He always wondered why Quinton had been so ready to relinquish the duties from this side of the business. Chaz had been more or less running the Black Diamond clubs for over a year, and when he'd asked Quinton to meet him, this seemed as good a place as any. He could see now that had been a mistake.

"Just look at those girls, at how young they are." Quinton set his jaw. "I should have sold this side of the business years ago, but hell if it wouldn't ruin my image to sell such a successful venture for *moral* reasons."

Chaz swallowed. "All of our girls are of age, sir, and they seem to really enjoy what they do. Frankly, with the impressive benefits package you provide them, they'd be hard pressed to find another job that could support their families."

Quinton released a hard breath and turned back to Chaz. "I don't want to talk about this pit anymore. Tell me about the ring. When are you planning to propose?"

"I'm just waiting for the right time, sir."

"Son, I'm not giving you the GM position. I'm bringing someone in from New York to be the general manager of Grand Escape."

Chaz sat back a little, reeling from the impact of Quinton's verbal punch. "I'm sorry to hear that. I think I could have—"

"The man I'm bringing in will do a fine job."

"I'm not doubting your judgment, sir."

"Spencer, I'm not just cutting down my workload for retirement. I need someone to oversee my whole company, and I want Carter Hotels and Entertainment to be in the hands of someone as ambitious as I am. Someone who has personal stakes."

Chaz licked his lips, daring to hope Quinton was headed in the right direction.

"I don't want you to be the Grand Escape GM, because I need you to run Carter Enterprises."

Chaz swallowed. "I would be honored."

Quinton held up a hand. "The job is only yours if you marry Riley. Like I said, I want my company to be operated by someone with a vested interest, and I want to know my daughter will never have to work as hard as I did. I'm not dead yet, and I can still run the business I built from nothing for several years now if I need to."

"I plan to marry Riley," Chaz assured him. Then, because he didn't want this to sound too much like the business decision it was, he added, "If she'll have me."

Quinton stood with a curt nod. "We'll talk again when there's a ring on my daughter's finger." With that, Quinton left the club.

Chaz's heart was pounding, his mouth watering at what was now within his grasp. Brandy caught his eye from across the room, her blond hair flashing in the club lighting. He winked at her. He was ready to celebrate.

...

CHARLIE WAS starting to think he was the womanizing ass the media made him out to be.

"I could get my own cab home," Riley said with a soft smile, but even as she said the words, she slid into the seat next to him.

The cab quickly filled with the scent of her—something soft and flowery that crept up on him anytime she was near. Sweet and feminine, it made him want to taste her. He hadn't been able to resist as they'd danced. He had simply surrendered to the impulse to skim his lips along the edge of her jaw, as he would if he were her lover.

"My mother taught me right," he said, hearing his own voice come out a little too gruff. "You gave me the pleasure of your company at dinner, and now I will see you to your door."

"Such a gentleman." She licked her lips innocently, and his gut clenched.

Did she realize she sat closer to him now, as they left the

restaurant, than she had on their drive here? He could feel the heat of her against his thigh. Did she have any idea how much he'd wanted her since the minute she'd walked out of her apartment sporting that black dress? Something about a dress that covered that much skin, it begged to be stripped from her hips.

What the hell was he doing? He *didn't* poach. Chaz was an ass—suspected and confirmed. Charlie'd taken Riley out tonight with every intention of nudging her to end things with him. But he didn't sleep with women who were deeply involved with other men—even if the other men were dicks who didn't know how to treat women.

Who was he kidding? Riley could be with Prince fucking Charming and he'd still think she was with the wrong guy. Because right now every cell in his body said that any man but him was all wrong for her.

He'd never enjoyed feeding a woman so much in his life. She'd gloried in each bite as if she hadn't tasted food in millennia. And the wine…God, the way she'd followed his instruction and let it sit in her mouth before she swallowed, her delicate throat working… and now her cheeks were flushed and a soft smile curved her lips as she wriggled lower in her seat, her hip rubbing his.

"Thank you for accompanying me tonight," he said. He curled his fingers into his own thigh to keep his hands in line, resisting the impulse to tuck back the loose wisps of hair at her temple.

She responded with a lazy smile. "*Hey,*" she said, the word long and slow, like a child pulling a piece of putty. "We never talked about Lacey's birthday."

Charlie tilted his head, studying her in the flicker of passing streetlights. "You're drunk."

She shrugged. "Not drunk, but not sober either." She snickered, then sank lower in the seat, leaning her head against his shoulder. "Just between you and me," she whispered, "I *like* not being sober."

Jesus. He hadn't done that on purpose. "Lightweight," he said, attempting to shift the growing sexual energy between them, to pretend she wasn't snuggling her body into his.

"My apartment's right up here," she said, tilting her chin up awkwardly to look in his eyes. "Hurry and tell me what you want to do for Lacey's birthday. What did you want to talk about?"

The driver pulled up to the curb by Riley's apartment, and Charlie handed him a wad of bills before guiding Riley out of the car. "Come on, princess. Time to get you to your castle before your date turns into a toad."

She giggled, following a step behind as he led the way into her complex. "I think you're mixing up your fairy tales."

Not at all, but he didn't need to share his impulse to act as King of the Pond Scum Kingdom right now. He *wanted* to take this little drunken flirtation and see how far she would take it. It was his nature. When he had a good hand, he played it, dammit. He didn't fold because of some busted sense of honor.

She took his arm as he headed up the stairs to her door, where he stopped, set his jaw, and leveled his gaze at the wooden apartment number. To look at Riley and not touch her was too difficult.

"Charlie?" She slid between him and her front door, squeezing his forearm. "Hey, did I do something wrong?"

She looked up at him with those big green eyes. She wouldn't stop him if he dipped his head to kiss her right now.

She wouldn't stop him, but she might hate him tomorrow.

"I have a confession," he said, forcing a smile. "I didn't really need to talk about my sister's birthday. I only wanted you to come to dinner with me. And you did, so…thanks."

She hadn't dropped her hand from his forearm and was drawing small circles there with her thumb. "I have a confession too," she said with a soft smile. "I figured that out about the time we pulled up to the restaurant."

He had to chuckle at that, if for no other reason than it let him off the hook a bit for acting like an enterprising jackass. "But you didn't demand I take you home."

"Charlie." Her gaze dropped to his mouth, and he thought, *Say good night, now.* But he stayed glued where he was, grateful as all hell when she rose up on her tiptoes and brushed her lips against his.

She was the one who started the kiss, but he was the one who finished it.

Before she could pull away, he plunged his hands into her hair, pulling more strands loose from her clip as he fought to hold on to her. He sipped at her lips first, tasting her sweetness. Then he slanted his mouth over hers. She opened under him. Let him kiss her. Kissed him like she was desperate to be kissed, swept her tongue inside his mouth as if she'd been thinking about this as much tonight as he had.

She pressed against his chest, then took fistfuls of his shirt, pulling him closer.

He slid a hand up her side until he was cupping the underside of her breast, and only at her soft moan did he pull away.

Eyes half closed, lips swollen, cheeks flushed, all framed by fallen locks of dark hair, she was the picture of beauty. She was everything he wanted, and everything he couldn't have.

"I should go," he said softly.

Her tongue darted across her lips. Was she tasting him there? "I'm sorry. That was a mistake. I shouldn't have—"

He put a finger to her lips. "Can we skip the conversation where we both apologize and take full responsibility for something neither of us is sorry happened?"

A soft puff of laughter escaped her lips. "See, Charlie Singleton, that's why I like you so much."

"Why's that?"

She shrugged. "You're not afraid to tell it like it is. You're the Devil himself, and making no excuses for it."

Charlie took a step back. "Good night, Riley."

"Good night."

He waited until she was in her apartment before he headed down the stairs. He was on the landing when she called to him.

"Charlie, wait!"

He turned to see her standing at the top of the stairs.

"He doesn't," she said. "He doesn't do any of those things for me." She took in a shaky breath. "And I don't know why I'm with him, but..." She looked away. "Maybe I shouldn't be."

CHAPTER
SEVEN

think *we should talk.*

Attempting a serious conversation with her boyfriend via text message probably wasn't the most mature thing she'd done. She sent the text in part to make herself stop lying in bed, wine warming her blood, thinking about *Charlie.* No doubt about it, the man made her wish she were the kind of woman willing to have a wild and reckless affair. She couldn't believe she'd kissed him.

She'd kissed another man. No, it was worse. She'd kissed another man and wished he hadn't stopped.

It was time to come clean with Chaz. She would start by admitting that there'd been something missing in their relationship.

Chaz's response came quickly. *What do you want to talk about?*

Her cheeks burned with shame. Never had she had to tell a man she'd been unfaithful, even to the most innocent degree. She would tell him. She would. If there was a *reason* to tell. But first she needed to know if there was any heat left between them.

Her thumbs hovered over the phone's keyboard. *Sex,* she finally typed.

On your mind too, huh?

She licked her lips. If there was even the slightest ember still burning between them, didn't she owe it to Chaz to see if she could get it blazing again? And what if she couldn't?

Much to her shame, her ING's instant answer to that question was a mental image of Charlie. The disintegration of her relationship with Chaz would mean a chance for that affair with Charlie. But was that really the kind of woman she was? Someone who preferred a hot affair to a lifetime of stability?

Why couldn't she get as excited about Chaz as she did about the bad boy who was no good for her?

Chaz's next message came before she had replied to his last:

Are you wearing it?

She glanced down. The oversized nightshirt was no black leather bustier.

No. Nothing that…interesting. Did you have a nice evening?

She put the phone back on her nightstand, closed her eyes, and pictured the way Charlie's eyes had turned hot as he'd fed her. In addition to a bottle of wine, she'd eaten most of his steak and very little of her own meal, and she couldn't deny that she'd been more turned on while Charlie slid a fork from her lips than she'd ever been lying under Chaz.

She needed to do something about that. Stat.

Her phone buzzed again.

Put it on.

She stared at the screen. This was Chaz. And this was what she wanted. Did he really want her to text him about putting on sexy lingerie?

Are you coming over? Maybe he didn't intend to text at all.

If you put on that leather get-up and tell me you want me there—me and not anyone else—I'll be over in a heartbeat.

Riley smiled and chewed on her bottom lip. She wished she *could* tell him that, but while her lips were still warm from Charlie's kiss, she knew it would be a lie. Besides, this was a side of Chaz she'd never seen before, and she liked it. She didn't want him to come to her apartment and freeze up. Instead, they could flirt like this and make her ING forget about Charlie Singleton.

And if she couldn't forget…she wasn't ready to go there yet.

Lacey was out for the night, and Riley had the apartment all to herself. Her ING purred as she stood and walked to her closet. Running a finger along the smooth leather, she imagined Charlie's smile as he'd bought it for her. Part of her wanted nothing more than to parade around in this for him. Her breathing accelerated, and she imagined him sitting in a chair as she strode in front of him. She'd saunter across the room, sway to some jazzy tune, and pass him long glances over her shoulder until he begged her to come to him.

She squeezed her eyes shut against the foolish fantasy—told herself it was probably a very bad idea to wear something for one man that made her think about another—but she pulled off the nightshirt in exchange for leather. She was lacing up the corset when her phone buzzed again.

Is it on?

She slipped into the red leather thong and nearly moaned. The leather was firm and unyielding, creating subtle, delicious friction as she moved.

I just need to add the matching red stilettos, she typed.

She pulled the shoes from the shelf and slid them on then stood to study herself in the mirror. Her skin was still flushed from the residual effects of the wine, and the pulse at her neck fluttered. The leather cups lifted her breasts, making them appear fuller than they were. Her phone buzzed.

By all means...

What now? she typed. Dear God. Was she really doing this? But she wanted to. She wanted to get her mind off Charlie Singleton as the cure to her sexual woes and explore a sexually fulfilling relationship with Chaz. She wanted something wild in her life, something fun and wicked. She wanted Charlie—no, *Chaz!*—to send her dirty text messages. She wanted him to tell her he was hard for her.

The phone buzzed in her hand, reminiscent of the vibrator in her drawer. A small smile curved her lips. What would Chaz think about that little toy?

She read the message.

Take a picture.

She swallowed hard. *Of…?*

You're not that naïve, Riley. I want a picture.

The next message came immediately after. *Use the mirror.*

She fumbled with the phone for a minute before figuring out how to use the camera.

She studied her reflection. As a final touch, she pulled the tie from her hair and let it tumble around her shoulders. Holding her breath, she held out her phone and took a picture of herself in the mirror.

Her finger hovered over the *Send* key, and her heart pounded. Would he like the way she looked? And why was she thinking about whether Charlie would approve of the way his gift hugged her body more than she was about Chaz's inclination toward leather?

"Just send it," she muttered, punching the button before she could talk herself out of it.

She stared at her phone. Nothing happened. She squeezed her eyes shut, wishing she could hit the universe's "undo" key. What the hell did she think she was doing?

Her phone buzzed and adrenaline pumped through her.

You just have no idea.

Then tell me.

It's a damn waste for you to be all alone wearing something that fucking sexy.

Her heart pounded. *So come over and keep me company.*

She gripped her phone. She hadn't just told him to come over, had she? Oh, Jesus. What if he did? Then this would end. He'd never talked to her like this in person, and she silently prayed he'd turn down her offer.

You have no idea how tempting that is. Do you really want me to?

She relaxed. *This is fun too.*

Afraid you'd do something you'd regret?

Regret? What did he think they would do? *I'd regret ending this conversation.*

I hate not being able to see you. I love watching you enjoy yourself.

She smiled. This was why she didn't want to end this. Chaz liked her, she knew that—otherwise, why would he waste his time with her?—but he wasn't one to *talk* about it. Having him talk about it made her feel good. *Not much to see. I'm just alone in my bedroom. Not like I'm touching myself or something.*

Well, why not?

Her mouth went dry. She settled onto her bed. *Because my hands are busy texting you.*

I wouldn't want you to stop doing that.

That's what I thought.

How's the leather feel?

Snug. Naughty. She chewed on her bottom lip and wriggled a little so the leather rubbed against her swollen clit. Had Chaz had some lingerie fetish this whole time and never told her?

Tell me what it makes you think about.

Charlie Singleton was probably not the response Chaz was looking for. Instead, she typed, *Hot, sweaty sex. Fast and desperate.*

Why do you hide this side of yourself?

She could ask him the same, but she didn't. In fact, she wasn't sure what to say, so she said nothing.

Do you have a small vibrator?

She giggled. *That's none of your business.*

Ahh, so that's a yes. Get it out and lie on your bed.

She opened her nightstand drawer and stared at the little bullet vibrator. She'd used the handy little toy, but never in the presence—phone, text, or otherwise—of Chaz or any other man.

Prop yourself up on some pillows and spread your legs.

Her mouth felt dry, but she wanted to follow his directions more than she wanted to quench her sudden thirst. She licked her lips as she sat on the bed and did as he directed.

I can't believe I'm doing this, she typed.

Slide the vibrator into your panties so it's nestled against your clit.

She closed her eyes, and her traitorous mind instantly conjured

Charlie's face, those intense eyes. She forced herself to picture Chaz, but couldn't help but give the smart retort she'd supply in a conversation with Charlie. *I know where it goes.*

Didn't know if you'd denied yourself that, too.

No. She didn't. Somehow, basic sexual pleasure had slipped through. *Don't be too excited. This won't be my first time.* But she'd never before used her vibrator under instruction from someone else.

Virgins are overrated.

She smiled at that.

Is it in your panties?

Riley instinctively squirmed at the delicious buzzing against her clit. She wasn't even touching it, wasn't moving it against herself, just letting it sit there, its rolling vibrations sitting against her sensitive skin.

It is. What about you?

I don't need a vibrator, baby.

Riley bit down on her lip, frowning. Baby? Chaz hadn't ever—to her recollection—called her that. But she liked it. *Is it*—how to ask this?—*in your hand?*

I need my hands to keep you on task.

She wanted him to call her, to make her brain accept that this was *Chaz* by hearing his voice. She wanted and she didn't want. If he called, it might get too real. Too…intimate? No, that couldn't be it. She might panic and never get to see what was at the end of this path.

I like to imagine you're enjoying this as much as I am, she typed, because knowing he was hot, knowing he was hard and ready—she couldn't imagine anything that could heighten these sensations more.

I swear that's the last thing you need to worry about.

She smiled and arched her back a little at the pleasure rolling through her. She imagined Chaz lying in bed, aroused. What would he do if he were here? Would he get her off? Would he want to watch her get herself off?

She couldn't imagine Chaz ever doing such a thing, but

somehow she sensed Charlie would like seeing her bring herself to orgasm. She closed her eyes. What did she have to do to get that man out of her mind?

Her phone beeped with a new message. *How does it feel?*

Good. Like a humming against my clit.

Slip your hand into your bustier and roll your nipple between your fingers.

She did it, squeezing her nipples between her fingers to the point of almost-pain. She rocked against the vibration between her legs, too swamped with pleasure to stop herself when it was Charlie, not Chaz, she imagined watching her. *Charlie* standing at the foot of the bed. *Charlie* with hot eyes on her. *Charlie* stroking himself as she writhed under the bullet's vibrations.

She forced her eyes open when the phone beeped again. She withdrew her hand from her the cup of the bustier to take the text.

Make yourself come for me.

The words shot a bolt of pleasure through her and she pressed the palm of her hand against her panties, pressing the vibrator against her clit and rocking against it and her hand through the waves of her orgasm. The whole time, an image of Charlie in her head.

She blinked. Charlie. This incredible experience with Chaz, and she'd been thinking about Charlie in every moment that counted.

...

RILEY SIPPED her coffee and flipped through the stack of paperwork on her desk. She was trying not to dwell too much on having been imagining Charlie throughout the only orgasm she'd ever shared with her boyfriend of two years, but it seemed too significant to ignore.

Her desk phone beeped and the light on the display let her know her father was paging her.

"Yes?"

"Riley, call HR and have them start on paperwork for the new general manager position."

She swallowed. "You've made your choice, then?" Though her father had general managers for his other hotels, he'd chosen to run his largest—Grand Escape—himself. But his retirement meant it was time to hire someone to take over that duty.

"Of course, and I think you'll approve."

Her heart lifted. He was announcing his retirement at breakfast tomorrow and she'd hoped she'd also announce he'd be giving the position to her. "Anyone I know?"

"I'm bringing in a gentleman from New York. Years of experience."

Riley slouched into her chair. "Oh. Okay." Her stomach pitched. Had she really thought he might give her the chance?

"I'm sure you'll still work by his side to make sure he settles in."

"Of course," she said, numbly.

The intercom clicked off and Riley sat, staring blindly at her dark computer screen.

"Riley?"

She looked up at her father, who had emerged from his office. "Yes?"

"You're not upset that I didn't give the position to you, are you? You know I can't have a woman running my company." He frowned. "It wouldn't be fair to you. Politically correct or not, this is a man's world, and it'd be harder for you."

She stared at him. He really felt that way.

"Listen." He lowered himself into the chair in front of her desk. "You're upset because you've been putting so much of your energy here, but once you start your family you'll be glad you don't have a hotel to manage."

"And who, exactly, will I be starting a family with?"

He chuckled. "I've let Chaz know that I approve of his decision to make your relationship more serious. You marry him and start a family." He rubbed his beard, ducking his head in a gesture that would have been best described as bashful on anyone else. "I'd like some grandkids, and I happen to know their mom doesn't need to worry about working a demanding job to make ends meet."

Riley softened. "You know how I feel about making it on my

own, Daddy."

He nodded. "I do. I know, but think how your life would have been different if your mother had accepted the money I offered her. You might feel differently when you have babies."

Something hard swelled in her throat, making it difficult to swallow. Her father leaned down and kissed the top of her head.

Riley watched her father retreat into his office, and her stomach sank. She'd given everything to this job. To him. She'd planned her life around it. And now he wanted her to be happy to sit back and marry a pre-approved suitor—a man whose face didn't even come to mind in her most erotic moments. He wanted her to have babies, and she wanted that too…just not yet.

With a single exception, she'd been the model child since Quinton Carter had taken her in. She'd always put on the perfect face for the media. What would her father think if he got wind of her dinner with a certain disreputable poker player?

Of course, he wouldn't need to know.

The receptionist, Lettie, came into the office smiling, and put a note on Riley's desk. "Chaz called," she said, grinning. "He wants you to meet him at The Orteja for lunch."

Riley raised a brow. "The Orteja? Are you sure?"

The receptionist's eyes lit up, and she pressed her hands against her chubby cheeks. "I listened to the message three times," she whispered.

Riley's mouth went dry as she gaped at the note. "I—" She licked her lips. When a girl found out that her boyfriend of two years had just made the biggest romantic gesture of their relationship, it didn't bode well if said girl's first thought was to hope that he wasn't proposing. "Thanks for the message."

"Riley!" her father boomed from his office. She darted to his office, imagining heart attacks and her father helpless on the floor.

Instead she found him standing at his desk, the newspaper in front of him unfolded to the society section. "Do I need to have my lawyer sue for this POS excuse for journalism?" His finger jabbed the page and Riley blinked at the spread of pictures. "Or did this really happen?"

EIGHT

"Bravo, my friend. Bravo."

Charlie rubbed his eyes and rolled over to look at the clock. Not even nine a.m. He hadn't slept for shit last night. Every time he'd closed his eyes, the image of Riley in skintight leather haunted him. But not as much as the image of her getting herself off while talking to him. So fucking hot.

He adjusted his cell phone against his ear and yawned for the benefit of his agent, who should have known better than to call before noon. "Bravo for what?"

"The photo op! The press just ate it up! Grab your *Las Vegas Times* and see for yourself."

"What photo—" He shot up in bed, remembering his directions to Rick. "Shit. You sent a photographer." He threw back the blankets and padded to the door of his suite. He snatched up the paper that waited just outside.

He dropped his phone in favor of tearing the paper open, and winced when he saw the front of the society page. The headline read: NATIONAL POKER PROFESSIONAL HAS LAS VEGAS'S GOOD DAUGHTER BETTING HER HEART. Under the headline were pictures capturing their night.

One shot showed Charlie dancing with Riley, his hand splayed possessively on her back while she looked up at him. Another showed him feeding her, and the photographer had caught the pleasure that shaped her features with each bite. But it was the final shot that made his gut burn. It showed Charlie at Riley's door, hands tangled in her hair as he kissed her.

"Fuck." He tucked the paper under his arm and snatched his phone from the floor. "They followed us after dinner?"

"And it paid off, didn't it? You did great. Now for the easy part. We'll just sit back and wait for the calls."

"I didn't tell you to have them follow us to her fucking apartment, Rick. *Jesus.*"

"What? You think I told them to do that? You know how these guys are. You give them an inch."

Charlie dragged a hand through his hair. This could work. He could get the sponsorship he needed, and Riley could get out of a bad relationship, but that didn't end the sick gnawing from growing in his gut. "Keep me posted, Rick."

He ended the call and stared at his phone for a long moment. He'd rather talk to Riley in person—or at the very least over the phone—but he didn't want to bother her at work again. He settled for a text.

Have you seen the paper?

He paced to his bedroom while he waited, throwing the newspaper on the desk and pulling some clothes from a suitcase. If all went well today, he'd have a sponsorship for the next tournament. And maybe the one after that.

If it didn't...well, Charlie should probably make himself a little more marketable by learning the Spanish translation for *Do you want fries with that?*

His phone beeped. *Yes. I'm so sorry. You must be angry.*

Why would he be angry? Did she think this was her fault? Shit, he should really tell her this was on him.

I'm just worried about you, he typed. A couple of innocent pictures had seemed so inconsequential when he'd suggested it to Rick yesterday, but after sharing last night with Riley, seeing their intimate moments exposed in print made him feel violated. Worse, it felt like the photographer had violated *her.*

Which was fucking convenient, since it was his own damn fault.

His phone beeped again. *Are you sure you still want to see me?*

Charlie shook his head in wonder as he thumbed his response.

Of course I do. After last night, seeing you in the flesh again is all I can think about.

...

THE ORTEJA was the kind of place where celebrities took in a late breakfast at one p.m. It was the kind of place where women met for three-martini lunches, and no one but a fool would think she could walk in off the street and be seated.

Riley sat alone at the table that had been reserved under Chaz's name and wondered if he'd had a change of heart. Ever since their text message conversation this morning, guilt had gnawed its pointy teeth into her conscience, curled its hairy tail around every thought.

Someone published pictures of her kissing another man, and he was *worried about her.* She didn't deserve anyone that wonderful. Particularly since, despite her best efforts, she still couldn't get her mind off a certain poker player.

Add the element of her father—furious, aghast... disappointed—and she could no longer deny that she'd made a mess of her tidy little life.

She checked the time on her phone. Twelve fifteen. Maybe Chaz had come to his senses and decided he didn't want anything to do with her. Drawing her bottom lip between her teeth, she clicked the command on her phone to send him a text.

I'm at The Orteja. I still want to see you if you want to see me.

I'm close. I can be there in five.

So he was still coming. Rolling her shoulders back, she took a sip of her water. She was determined not to be critical. Chaz had proven that he trusted her. That he cared for her even if she wasn't perfect. Even if she made mistakes. It was high time she returned the favor.

She blinked when, less than a minute later, Chaz came through the door with a bouquet of white roses. As he crossed to her, a string quartet gliding behind him, their bows working beautiful melodies from their instruments.

Her pulse skittered to a pause and air refused to enter her lungs.

Chaz dropped to his knee in front of her. The quartet decrescendoed as he pulled something from his pocket.

Riley crossed her arms, and her stomach lurched. Everyone around them had stopped their conversations and turned from their drinks to stare.

"Riley Elaine Carter," Chaz said, opening a black velvet box, "we love each other."

She swallowed hard, eyes darting to the spectators around them. She willed him to stop, willed time to go in reverse so she could cancel this meal. He'd never taken her to The Orteja. She should have known.

"I know last night was just your way of getting my attention. Of getting me to ask you the question I should have asked you months ago." He gave a sheepish grin. "I think I've just been too afraid to change something so...perfect."

Riley winced. How could she put a stop to this? "Chaz—"

"You are the woman I want to talk to when life gets hard. You're the woman I want to raise my children."

Bile rose in her throat. Did he want a wife or a nanny?

He lifted the box and Riley winced at the size of the diamond. Square cut and at least three carats, the stone leered at her more than winked. "I'm ready to marry you."

Riley blinked. Wait. Wasn't he supposed to *ask*...? Chaz stood and drew her from her chair and into his arms. Applause erupted, as the crowd around them stood. Over Chaz's shoulder, one man wasn't clapping.

"Charlie?"

He stood, arms dropped to his sides, stance wide. Their gazes locked for a long moment before he gave her a curt nod and turned away.

"About those pictures…" Chaz whispered in her ear, "I'm going to let you make it up to me."

He held her tight but she managed to wriggle her hands between their bodies and press against his chest. He took a step back, smiling down at her but not releasing her.

"Can we go somewhere…private to talk?"

The smile dropped from his face for a beat before he carefully replaced it. "Sure. Anything for my fiancée." He wrapped a possessive arm around her shoulder and winked to the crowd. "Apparently the lady wants me alone."

The crowd's laughter was another punch in Riley's already roiling stomach. She couldn't do this. She didn't want to be this close to Chaz. If she wanted to shove him off her because he was holding her close, how was she supposed to marry him?

When they cleared the restaurant doors, he released her shoulders but resumed his possessive hold on her upper arm. "You almost embarrassed me in there." He smiled, but it didn't reach his eyes.

"Can we just…go to my office and talk?"

"Sure."

"And let go of my arm. You're hurting me."

He released her instantly. "Sorry." Again the forced smile. "I think after those pictures in the paper this morning, I feel like I have to hold on to you or I might lose you."

They walked the two blocks back to Grand Escape in stiff silence. The Las Vegas heat pounded them, and with each step Riley grew angrier. Didn't she deserve a man whose idea of a wife was more than a job description for a nanny? Didn't she deserve a man who would be hurt if she kissed another man? Who was passionate enough about their love to scream about it? Yes. She did.

And she deserved to be *asked* for her hand in marriage, not told she was going to give it.

When they stepped into the Grand Escape lobby, the air conditioning felt like a freezer against her dewy skin, and it only hardened her resolve.

Chaz approached the elevator and she stopped short. "You know I can't take that," she whispered.

"Get over it, Riley. It will be fine."

She winced. "Do you even care what I feel about *anything*?"

His eyes turned darker, harder. "You apparently rode in an elevator last night, or that photographer wouldn't have been able to take pictures of you at the Eiffel Tower Restaurant."

"That was different. I—" What? She'd been with Charlie Singleton? She'd had his arm around her, his breath brushing across her ear as she'd faced her fear? "It's different in a glass elevator. I can do a glass elevator."

He punched the button. "Then you can do this one too."

Riley stared after Chaz as the elevator doors slid open and he walked in without her. He leaned against the wall and looked at her until the doors slid closed again.

She closed her eyes and wished with all her might that she wasn't such a coward.

By the time she climbed the twenty-two flights of stairs to her office, Chaz was showing off her ring to Lettie.

"There she is," Chaz said when he spotted her. He gave her a tight smile and tucked the ring into his pocket. "Hold Ms. Carter's calls, please," he requested. "My fiancée and I need some alone time."

She made sure her office door was firmly shut behind her before she turned to Chaz and braced her hands on her hips. "I wish you'd quit calling me that!"

Chaz straightened his shoulders and puffed out his chest. "What are you talking about?"

Riley couldn't help but mentally tally all the ways he came up short when compared with Charlie. Charlie's shoulders were broader, his chest better defined, his biceps thicker.

Charlie would have taken the freaking stairs with her.

"I'm not your fiancée, Chaz. So quit telling everyone I am."

His scowl drew his features tight and made him look more like a spoiled child than a confident man. "We just got engaged. Last I checked, that makes you my fiancée."

"You're being deliberately obtuse. I never agreed to anything."

His body deflated. His shoulders sagged and he blew out a breath before collapsing into a chair. He ran a hand through his hair. "I've screwed this all up," he said softly, his eyes downcast.

"No, you haven't. It's just—" She put her hand to her mouth, fighting the instinct to comfort him.

"Did you know I've been planning this proposal for weeks?"

She blinked. He'd been planning a proposal while she'd been trying to decide whether their lack of sex life was reason enough to end the relationship. The revelation made her feel small.

"And then this morning, the day I've been planning, I'm making final arrangements when I see pictures of the woman I love kissing some gambler."

A professional poker player was a far cry from a gambler, but she didn't dare say so when shame was smacking her in the face.

He looked up at her, his cool blue eyes searching her face. "So if I came across heavy-handed, if this didn't go quite as I planned… could you cut me some slack?"

Her jaw worked, but she couldn't find the words. She'd wanted this for so long. She'd been ready—anxious, even—to move forward. Why was she so fast to throw it away?

"I'm sorry I pushed you to get on the elevator. I'm just…hell, I'm jealous you'd do it for some other guy." He shook his head. "So I was an ass. I'm sorry."

He stood and walked slowly to her, retrieving the ring box from his pocket. He slid the ring from the case and took her hand.

"Riley," he said, sliding the ring on her finger, "be my wife."

Her hand shook. "I can't," she whispered.

"Shh." He put a finger to her lips. "You don't have to answer yet. You're confused. I understand that. You don't have to say *yes* yet, but don't throw this away by saying *no*."

She wriggled the ring off her finger and offered it to Chaz. "This ring is a promise," she said.

"It's my promise to you." He closed her fingers around the hard rock and platinum band. "I might not be as exciting as a world-traveling poker player, but I can give you a good life."

"Wearing it is a promise too, and I can't promise you anything in return," she said softly. "Not right now." The words hurt. They tore at the heart of the little girl inside her—the little girl who'd lost her only family at twelve and had to move in with a man she didn't know, the little girl who wanted only to be loved unconditionally and have the stable family she'd only dreamed of.

"He might be exciting, but you know what I am? I'm patient, Riley. I'm willing to wait for what I want."

CHAPTER
NINE

No matter how hard Charlie went at the bag in Grand Escape's state-of-the-art fitness center, he couldn't shake the feeling that he'd just been royally screwed.

Why had she invited him there? Had she known Chaz would be proposing? Had she wanted him to see? When she'd looked at him over Chaz's shoulders, there had been something in her eyes that had made him draw up short. She'd had the look of a deer in the headlights—frozen, unsure whether to run or fight, and doing neither.

He punched the bag harder, sweat dripping down his forehead and off his chin, but it didn't change the fact that Riley hadn't told Chaz *no*.

"Need someone to hold that for you?"

Charlie glanced over his shoulder to see a kid in basketball shorts and a t-shirt. Dark, long, and lanky, he reminded Charlie a lot of himself as a teen. Charlie rolled his shoulders back. If he weren't already wiped, he'd have refused the kid. He'd have to pull his punches so the teen could keep hold of the bag. "Sure."

The kid exuded confidence as he stepped behind the bag. The way Charlie had been whaling on the thing, it'd be smart to show a little caution. "What's got you so pissed off?"

"What?" Charlie wiped his brow and realized his knuckles were sore. He'd been going at the bag bare-fisted because it was more satisfying, but he'd pay for it later. "Why do you think I'm pissed? Maybe I'm just working out."

The kid arched a brow. "I've seen guys hit the bag before. Sometimes it's just a bag, and sometimes the guy wishes it was someone's face. Pretty easy to tell which is which."

Charlie threw a test punch at the bag and nodded in approval as the kid held it steady. *Jab, cross, jab, jab!* "You're perceptive," he said, stepping back. *Jab, cross, kick, jab!* "And pretty strong for a kid."

"I'm sixteen," the kid said.

Charlie raised a brow. *Jab, cross, uppercut.*

"It seems young to you now, but you didn't think of yourself as a kid when you were my age. You were only a year older than me when you ran off to LA."

Charlie stepped back and rubbed his knuckles. "What do you know about me?" He stepped around the bag and nodded for the kid to take a turn. Charlie held the bag while the kid threw steady and intentional punches.

"You're Charlie Singleton," the kid said after a round. "'The Devil,' right? I know a lot about you just from watching ESPN2."

Charlie frowned. *The Devil.* He hated that damn nickname. "Well, don't believe everything you see on TV."

"I heard you're being sued for child support."

Charlie shoved the bag and stepped back. "What's it to you?"

The kid lifted a shoulder. "Do you think he's yours?"

"Anything is possible." Charlie took a second look at the kid. Sixteen. Dark hair. Tall, athletic. Cocky.

"You even want anything to do with him if he is?"

Charlie crossed his arms. "What'd you say your name was?"

The kid blinked and looked to the ceiling for a split second. "Derrick."

"*Derrick*, it's complicated. No one ever told me I had a kid, and I'm not exactly role model material."

"Derrick" took position behind the bag and nodded for Charlie to take a turn. "So that gets you out of it? Not your fault, so you can just walk away?"

Charlie worked the bag for a few before answering. "I didn't say I was going to walk away." He lifted his eyes to meet the kid's. Blue, just like his own. Go figure. "Sticking around might not be the best thing for this kid. I have to consider that."

The kid shrugged as if Charlie's answer meant nothing to him. "That's cool." He looked at his watch. "Hey, I've gotta bounce."

Charlie nodded, something painful balling in his throat. "Thanks for the company."

The kid grinned. "It's a woman, isn't it?"

"What?"

"The reason you were so pissed. Only a woman can rile a guy up like that and make him choose to hit a bag instead of someone's face."

Laughter slipped from Charlie's lips and he found himself grinning.

"Just don't be like those idiots in the movies and let everything fall apart because you're too afraid to tell her the truth about how you feel."

Charlie raised a brow. "A sage at sixteen?"

The kid lifted his palms in a what-can-you-do gesture. "Women are my specialty," he said before turning to the door.

"Hey, kid!" Charlie called after him. "Derrick" stopped and looked over his shoulder. "I'll be here tomorrow, same time." He wasn't sure why he said it, but the words were out of his mouth before he could analyze his reasons.

The kid nodded slowly. "Yeah. That could be all right."

...

"I HAVE never seen my brother look at a woman like that." Lacey stared at the paper, eyes wide. Riley plopped down on the couch next to her and Lace reiterated, "*Ever.*"

"Lace—"

"It's not like he's never been in a relationship, but—"

"Lacey!"

She bit her lip. "I'm sorry. It's cute."

"Chaz took me to lunch at The Orteja today."

"Yikes, was he mad? Shit. What'd you tell him? That kiss"—she dropped her eyes to the paper—"shit, he's gotta be upset. I've never seen *him* kiss you like that, and I'm not even sure he's—"

"Lace, he proposed."

"—capable." She stopped. "Oh."

Riley let out a breath. "Right. Exactly."

"So." Lacey chewed her bottom lip.

"So?" Riley winced. "A girl's best friend should be happy when her boyfriend proposes."

Lacey nodded. "Right! Oh, yeah. Of course." She leaned forward and gave Riley a light hug.

Riley pulled back. "You don't have to fake it, Lacey."

The strained smile dropped off Lacey's face. "I don't?"

"I didn't say *yes*."

Lacey's blue eyes lit up. "You said *no*?"

"Not exactly."

She frowned. "What does that mean? And does Charlie know?"

"It means that I wasn't ready to say *yes*, but I wasn't ready to give up on our relationship either. And yes, Charlie knows. He happened to be at The Orteja when Chaz dropped to a knee."

"Ouch."

Riley closed her eyes. She couldn't tell Lacey the truth—that she was grateful for Charlie's presence. The man she wanted had watched as the man she was supposed to want offered her a ring. His presence reminded her not to settle.

"Listen, our lease is up in a couple months, and I know I'd kind of indicated that I'd like to get my own place."

Lacey nodded. "I understand, Ry. We can't live like we're in college forever. Plus, when you get the GM position, you'll be raking in the cash. You won't need to live here."

Riley wrung her hands. "My father gave that position to someone else."

Lacey gaped. "He didn't!"

"I'm sorry to say it's true."

"Well, that's his loss, Riley, because you would have made the best GM Grand Escape had ever seen."

Riley looked into her friend's eyes. She was so grateful to have Lacey. "I don't know if that's true, but it's really irrelevant. My father doesn't want me in management. He wants me married and out of the corporate world." She squeezed her eyes shut. "I can't believe I never saw it before, but he could have had me working any number of places in that hotel that would have better prepared me for the job. Instead, he kept me by his side working as a glorified secretary. I thought it was so he could show me the ropes, but he really just wanted to keep an eye on me."

Lacey didn't reply.

Riley had to close her eyes. At twenty-six years old, she should have started making her own decisions a long time ago rather than allowing her father to make them for her. "You knew, though, didn't you?"

When she opened her eyes again, Lacey was biting her lip.

Riley shook her head. "It's okay. I can see it now." She could also see that her father was trying to transfer the reins of her life to Chaz.

"I'm sorry, Riley," Lacey whispered.

Riley shrugged. "It's not your fault."

"How could he—"

She held up her hands before her friend began a speech in her defense. "That doesn't matter now. I'm done being controlled. I have some money saved up, and—if you'll still be my roommate—I can start looking for a new job where I'm just me, not somebody's daughter."

"What about dance?" Lacey asked softly.

Riley reached over and squeezed her friend's hand. "It's sweet of you to suggest it, but I don't think I have what it takes to make it in that world." Riley wrapped her arms around her friend. "Thanks. For everything." On the table, her phone buzzed.

Lacey sniffed. "I'm the one who should be thanking you."

"So you'll put up with me for another year?" Riley asked.

Lacey laughed. "As long as you want. Now I'll leave you alone. I think someone's trying to get a hold of you."

Riley snatched her phone from the table. She had a message from Chaz. She frowned. She knew she was asking a lot after he put himself out there today, but she needed some space before she could make a decision.

She opened the message: *Tell me the truth. What did last night mean to you?*

...

C<small>HARLIE DIDN'T</small> know what the hell he was doing. He didn't have anything to offer Riley. He'd show her respect and affection, sure, but for what? A week before he left town again? On the other hand, any internal conflict he had about talking Riley out of marrying Chaz was laid to rest when he remembered the way Chaz had acted at the Black Diamond yesterday.

Charlie might not know much about love and lasting relationships, but he knew that if Riley was going to have one, she deserved someone a hell of a lot better than that.

His phone beeped and he found himself half surprised she'd responded. Newly engaged, she wouldn't have been wrong to ignore him. *Which part?*

He winced. He wanted to believe the whole night had meant something to her, but maybe for Riley their messages had been nothing but cheap, modern-day phone sex. If their erotic texts had meant nothing, he didn't want to know it. *Start with dinner.*

It was supposed to be innocent. But then it became something more. That's why I can't wear that ring.

Charlie straightened. Holy shit. She wasn't wearing the ring. Had she refused Chaz? And had she done it for Charlie?

He should call her. This conversation was too important to have over text messages. No, even the phone wasn't good enough. *I think we should talk.*

I just need time. I'm not ready to make a decision yet.

Charlie closed his eyes. There was a God. Good. *You should take your time. The man who marries you is the luckiest guy on earth. You should make sure he's worthy.*

Your texts are so sweet and…sexy. This decision would be easier if I believed we could be like this face to face.

Come over and let me prove we can. He was sure there was a special place in hell for men preparing to seduce another man's almost-fiancée, but Charlie would happily burn there to spend a night proving to Riley that she deserved better than Chaz.

I'm just confused right now, her next message said, and Charlie figured that made two of them. The message after that knocked him on his ass.

I love you.

CHAPTER
TEN

Riley took a fortifying breath when she reached Chaz's condo. He'd never responded to her last text.

I love you.

She wasn't even sure if she meant the words anymore, but saying them—typing them—had been a testament to her decision to give their relationship a chance until she could make a decision about his proposal. Why did he seem like a completely different person when they exchanged text messages? And why couldn't he be more of that person when they were together?

She rolled back her shoulders. Just because things had never been hot between her and Chaz didn't mean they couldn't be. She'd never fought to make their sex life better than it was. She'd been a coward, but not anymore.

She knocked and waited. Nothing.

The windows were dark. Should she have called? Had he gone to bed? She'd wanted to surprise him. She'd dressed in a black skirt and halter, an outfit that revealed more than her normal choices. She'd never dressed like this for him because she hadn't thought he'd like it. But then she hadn't thought he'd like black leather lingerie either, and look where that had gotten them.

She knocked again and put her ear by the door, listening for the sound of footsteps. Nothing.

She could call him. But maybe he'd gone to bed and this was her chance to slip under the sheets with him and wake him up in a much more interesting way. Why didn't the idea appeal to her more? This was her potential future-fiancé. She shouldn't be mildly put off by the idea of waking him up with her body.

She held her breath and turned the knob, hoping he might have kept it unlocked.

When it turned and the door opened, apprehension rose up in her. She was really going to do this.

She and Chaz had had sex plenty of times, but this was different. This would change everything between them. At least she hoped…

From the door, she could hear the music pulsing from the bedroom. She frowned and followed the sound, walking through the great room. Maybe he'd been getting things ready for her and hadn't heard her knock. She turned into the bedroom and froze.

A blonde was on all fours in the middle of the bed and Chaz was behind her, guiding her hips as he took her from behind. He was so lost in his own pleasure, he didn't even notice Riley until the laughter bubbled from her lips.

She didn't bother watching him scramble as she let herself out, giggles racking her body, edging closer to hysteria with every step. She'd wanted some excitement in their love life and her wish had been granted.

"Riley!"

She'd almost made it out the door when his fingers wrapped around her arm. "Fuck off, Chaz." The words felt strange in her mouth—foreign—but delicious.

"I can explain."

She shook her head. "No need. What, did you want me to join you? Or am I just supposed to stand aside while you give *her* all your sexual energy and screw me like a puritan?" She yanked her arm from his grasp.

"You're angry. I get that. But cool off, and tomorrow we'll talk."

Another bout of laughter seized her. She snorted. She didn't realize she was crying until she felt the tears on her cheeks.

"I'm sorry," he whispered. "She's nothing to me. Just some woman I met in the casino. Just a good time to burn off some energy."

Her laughter tasted bitter on her tongue. "What about the texts, huh, Chaz?"

He pulled a hand through his dark hair. "Seriously? You're angry that I forgot to send you a *text message*? I was busy tonight."

She released a puff of air. "I can see that."

"Listen, I'm not sure why you came over like this, but did you think maybe you should call first?"

Her jaw worked, but she couldn't find words. He was angry. As if *he'd* been wronged.

"Riley, I proposed to you today and you turned me down, so don't make me out to be some asshole."

"I said I needed *time*." She looked up, willing her tears to hold off another minute. "Whatever this was between us, it's over."

He pulled a hand through his dark hair. "You don't understand. There are some things a man wants to do, *urges* that he has he doesn't want to satisfy with the future mother of his children."

She flinched at that twist of the knife. "Aren't you talking out both sides of your mouth now? You did it because I won't marry you, but I'm going to be the mother to your children?"

"Won't you be, Riley? Eventually?"

The blonde emerged from the bedroom, a gold satin robe wrapped around her.

"I can't talk about this right now," Riley said, because the last thing she wanted was to have this conversation while looking at the woman with whom Chaz *wanted* to satisfy his "urges."

She needed to call a cab. She was out on the sidewalk, reaching for her cell when it rang. *Call from Charles Spencer.*

"Leave me alone. I don't want to talk to you right now." She hated the sound of her voice—shaky and pathetic as her chest shook with her tears.

"Whoa! Hold up. What happened? Did I miss something?"

A sense of calm washed over her. That wasn't Chaz's voice. It was Charlie's.

...

I LOVE *you.*

Charlie frowned and paced through his suite. What the hell had just happened? Why was she pissed? "Riley, tell me what just happened."

I love you.

She wasn't the first woman to spring those words on him, so he shouldn't be surprised.

She's the first woman you liked *hearing it from,* a voice in his mind nudged.

He shifted on the couch in his suite and waited for her explanation to the rapid change in her attitude. Maybe she was embarrassed she'd typed the words at all, and now she was taking that out on him.

"Charlie?" she said, and his name sounded like a question.

"What's going on, Riley?" Because, hell, he deserved to know. He'd been pushing it by asking her to come to him, but he couldn't go to her. He needed to know that *she* wanted this as much as he did. He'd needed her to make a move live and in person, because his male ego refused to continue playing second fiddle to some other guy.

I love you.

Fuck it. He needed her to come to him because he wanted to believe someone like Riley could love someone like him.

"Holy crap," she whispered. "I—I'm sorry. I thought you were Chaz."

"Chaz…your boyfriend?" So that was why she hadn't come over. She was busy fighting with that idiot—a fight that had her in tears from the sound of it. That just went to show Chaz was too damn important to her for Charlie's peace of mind.

"He's not my boyfriend. Not anymore."

He collapsed on the couch, leaning his head back and grinning. "Good to hear you say it."

"Did you…" She took in a shaky breath. Tears were making her voice thick. "Tonight? Oh, Jesus, *last night*. Our text messages? They were…"

"Special?" he supplied. "Sexy? Wicked hot?" He felt his lips twist into a grin. "And, tell me if I'm on target with this last one, but I was going for *orgasmic*."

She laughed, and Charlie relaxed—Chaz or no, there was nothing he enjoyed more than making this woman smile.

"Tell me about your fight with Chaz," he said, then wished he hadn't. He didn't need to get himself involved in their relationship. He didn't have the heart not to paint Chaz as the bad guy in any scenario, partly because it was likely the truth and partly because Charlie was a selfish ass who wanted Riley to himself.

I love you.

Yes, he wanted her for himself, and that want was made all the more intense by her feelings for him. If Riley had fallen for him, she must have seen him as more than the womanizer she'd accused him of being. She must have seen him for more than the kid from the wrong side of the tracks who had some luck at the poker table.

Her sigh was heavy, and Charlie found himself wondering if it was confusion or regret weighing it down. "I don't think Chaz is the man I thought he was."

"We rarely are," he said softly, his eyes drifting to the subpoena papers on his desk. If Angela had really known what kind of man Charlie was, she wouldn't have bothered with this legal bullshit. If she'd had a clue what he was about, she would have owned up to the secret she'd kept from him for sixteen years and asked him to do the tests. "Anything specific bring this to your attention?"

"I don't want to talk about it right now," she said.

"What do you want to talk about?"

"I don't want to talk at all. I just want…I want to stop being a coward."

"Riley, you are no coward. In fact, you're—"

"I have to go, Charlie." The line went dead, and Charlie was left cussing at an empty room.

He pulled a hand over his face. She had him tied up in knots, and for the first time in his life, he wasn't sure what to do next.

He looked at the papers from Angela. It had been interesting meeting "Derrick" today. Riley wasn't the only part of his life where he'd been dealt a hand he wasn't sure how to play, and every good poker player knows decisions need to be made with confidence.

Five minutes later, his phone beeped, alerting him to a text message. *I'm downstairs.*

His stomach clenched. Riley. God, every time he pictured her face, he grew hard, still imagining her placing the vibrator between her legs last night. He liked knowing she'd been thinking of *him*, not some asshole kind-of boyfriend, when she came.

And now she was here.

CHAPTER
ELEVEN

"I was going to come to your room," Riley whispered to Charlie when the elevator doors opened.

She'd grabbed a key from housekeeping that would get her into Charlie's suite, because the elevators wouldn't go to the penthouse floors without it. Stairs weren't an option. She was able to take the stairs to her office every day because, in the executive tower, the alarm wasn't programmed to sound if the stairs were used. In the penthouse tower, on the other hand, the standard automatic door alarm was still engaged. Those stairs were for fire escape only. Opening the doors would wake every living creature in the place...probably some dead ones too.

She looked at Charlie's face. His soft smile, those ice-blue eyes turning darker as he stared at her. This was about more than a fire alarm.

Riley had wasted two years betting everything on a man who had offered nothing in return, and seeing him with that woman hurt. But she'd also been a little...relieved.

When Charlie called her and she realized her phone had been mis-programmed, she'd wanted to come here; she'd wanted to prove to herself that she could be wild, that she could live in the moment just once.

She'd come knowing she'd have to get in that elevator. She'd come wanting to face that almost as much as she wanted to be with Charlie.

"I don't want to be afraid anymore," she said.

From inside the elevator, Charlie extended a hand.

She shook her head. "But I am," she whispered. "I want to so much. But I can't."

"Look at me."

His oxford shirt was unbuttoned at the collar and he'd rolled his sleeves to his elbows, exposing thick, muscular forearms.

He was beautiful—sexy, with hungry eyes that devoured her from where he stood. The way he looked at her—ran his eyes over her, lingering on her hips, her breasts—was erotic, and every bit as effective as if his fingers touched each place his eyes lingered.

During their short phone conversation, her sluggish brain had clicked together all the pieces and rewritten history—sexy texts in her office from *Charlie*, instructions to touch herself with her vibrator from *Charlie*.

The decision to come to him—to *be with him*—had been the easiest Riley had ever made.

It was a damn shame the elevator stood between her and that objective.

Charlie took a step forward. Framed by the elevator's gaping mouth, he pressed one hand against the door and extended the other to her.

She looked into his eyes and took his hand. She could do this.

She stepped into the elevator and jumped as the doors slid closed behind her.

"You are so much braver than you think," he said, his breath against her ear.

The space was too small. The walls too solid. There wasn't enough room.

"Riley, close your eyes."

She gasped and blinked. There wasn't enough air. She had to get out.

She eyed the ceiling for the panels people always climbed

through in the movies, but when she lifted her gaze, the ceiling dropped two feet closer to her head. Her stomach pitched.

"Close your eyes, Riley."

She couldn't breathe. Air wasn't entering her lungs. She clawed at the neckline of her shirt. She had to—

Charlie's warm hand slid under her shirt and he pulled her back against him. "Relax."

"I can't relax. You don't understand. I'm—"

He swept her hair over her shoulder and pressed his mouth her neck. "Close your eyes for me." His voice was deeper, softer, his breath against her ear.

She let her lids drift closed and irrationally wished he had done this in her office earlier. Her office, the hall, the restaurant, the middle of the street—anywhere but closed up and trapped inside this—

"Whatever you're thinking about, stop. You're not doing yourself any favors."

"What...what do you want me to think about?" she asked, feeling her panic rise again. She kept her eyes closed. If she couldn't see the walls, she could breathe. She couldn't risk opening them now.

He slid his hand further around her, circled her navel with his thumb. "Think of something that relaxes you," he said, moving his hand to brush the underside of her breasts. "Think of why you came to me. And relax."

Oh, boy. *This* certainly didn't relax her. Her pulse spiked but not in the thready, panicked way of ninety seconds ago. This was a powerful spike. The kind that sent signals to the brain to pump more blood and to pump it all to her breasts, nipples, and the sweet, hungry spot between her legs—ASAP.

"What makes your mind go blank and your muscles turn to jelly?"

His mouth traced the line of her neck. Not kissing, exactly, not even tasting. More like sampling the texture of her skin. The action made her feel beautiful and wanted. Heat pooled low in her belly, followed by moisture between her legs.

"God, you smell good," he whispered against her ear.

Suddenly, she was against the wall and Charlie's mouth was on hers.

Her fingers curled into his biceps.

His tongue slipped past her lips and his thumb traced the edge of her jaw. Her shoulders relaxed, and she opened under him, turned into the kiss, and tasted him.

Charlie tasted of breath mints and hot, delicious male. And as he kissed her—*God*, could he kiss—bubbles of nervous pleasure tickled her belly and spread a shiver all the way to her fingertips.

She slipped her hands to his waist and yanked his shirt from his jeans. She wanted to feel the heat of his skin, wanted to scrape her nails over that taut stomach. Hell, she wanted to go further south, but she'd take this as a starting point.

"Riley." His breath was hot against her ear as he spoke. "We're here." His hand was on her breast now, his thumb teasing her nipple through her bra.

"Mmm," she said, because she didn't care about the elevator door anymore. She cared about Charlie and how good he tasted and how soon she could test the fit of his cock in her hand. She cared about leaving Chaz and coming to Charlie. She cared about feeling alive.

She fumbled for the button on his slacks.

"Riley." Her name was more groaned than said.

He pulled her hands from his waistband and wrapped them around his neck. His mouth took hers, hard, desperate. His hand slid up the inside of her thigh and her hips instinctively rocked toward him.

He rubbed her through her panties. She buried her face in his neck and rocked against him, somehow channeling all the energy from her fear into desire.

He slid his fingers under the lace, and she clung to him. She was slick with need and he slid over her clit and back. She arched, pressed into him, willing him to slide inside her.

When he finally dipped a finger inside her, her own gasp of pleasure mingled with his groan.

"God, you feel good," he whispered, his breath hot against her ear.

She clung to him, latched on to his neck and sucked while her hands clawed at his back. She rocked into his hand, let him fuck her with his fingers.

She wanted more. So much more. "Get inside of me," she whispered. It was need—and fear, and confusion, and a horrible feeling that her life wasn't in her control after all—that had her making this request.

"Here?" His voice was rough, like it'd been dragged over the ragged edges of need. "You're sure?"

"Now," she said. "Please."

She thought he'd pull her panties to the side and slide into her quickly, take her fast and hard against the wall. She was surprised when he dropped to his knees and gently peeled the red lace from her hips. One at a time, he lifted her feet and helped her step out of her panties.

She made the mistake of taking her focus off him, the mistake of looking to the opposite wall of the elevator. "Oh, shit," she whispered, her heart lurching.

"Look at me, Riley," Charlie said, still on his knees.

She looked down into those blue eyes gazing up at her like she was a goddess.

Bunching her skirt around her waist, he pressed his mouth between her legs, licked, kissed, sucked.

The world reeled.

She fisted her hands in his hair. She'd always loved the feeling of a man's tongue against her sex, but Chaz didn't like going down on her. She'd never pressed the issue, but God had she missed it. She didn't even realize how much until she felt Charlie's mouth on her.

She opened her eyes to take in the sight of him kneeling before her, the erotic image of his face buried between her legs. He was sliding a condom on while he worked her with his mouth.

"That's what I call multitasking," she whispered.

He chuckled and slowly stood, keeping a hand between her

legs. "I could taste you for hours," he whispered as he fondled her.

She kissed him and tasted herself on his lips. "Play your cards right and maybe someday I'll let you," she whispered.

"I'm damn good with cards," he said, sliding his hands behind her ass and lifting her. "So don't make any bet you can't make good on." With that, he settled her on the long, hard length of his cock.

She pressed herself against the wall, rocking her hips into him as he filled her, wanting to be impossibly close to him. His fingers dug into her hips, guiding her through to meet his rhythm.

"You feel so good," he whispered against her ear, and the words made her clench around him. She circled her hips to feel the rub of her clit against him, and he pulled back, withdrawing almost all the way before bringing her down again.

The head of his cock pressed against her cervix, making her moan and hold him deep inside.

When she came, it wasn't in a blinding flash of light but in pulsing ripple of pleasure. Her orgasm rolled out from her core in waves.

He pressed his mouth to hers, kissed her as he pumped his hips and followed her orgasm with his own.

...

CHARLIE COULDN'T believe he was holding this beauty in his arms. He looked down at Riley's flushed cheeks and unwrapped her legs from his waist. He adjusted her clothes, covering her, and did the best he could with the condom.

Riley blinked up at him, pulling her bottom lip between her teeth as she steadied herself on her feet.

"You watched me dance," she said, her words so soft he almost couldn't hear them.

Charlie hit the button on the elevator to make the doors open. "What?" As he waited for the metal doors to slide apart, he was struck with the reality of what he'd just done.

What would have happened if someone from a lower floor had been waiting for an elevator? His first time with Riley could have ended in disaster, and that wasn't what he wanted her remembering.

He cursed himself for his carelessness.

"Yesterday before dinner," she said. He led her out of the elevator and into his suite. "You sent me texts saying you watched me dance."

He couldn't help but smile. It was a nice memory. She didn't have the typical dancer's body—lithe with minimal breasts and no hips. Riley's curves made her movements all the more beautiful, all the more seductive. "I liked watching you. Did you mind?" he finally asked.

She frowned. "Why would I mind? It was…"

When it seemed as if she didn't plan to finish her sentence, he tipped up her chin and looked into her eyes, his heart tight. "Tell me."

"It made me feel like I matter."

Internally, he winced. He understood her statement even if he wanted to protest. For too much of his life, moments of feeling significant were few and far between. Who knew rich heiresses could feel the same way? "You do. More than you know."

He dipped his head to sip at her lips.

His cell rang, and Charlie fished it out of his pocket and threw it on the floor, never taking his lips from hers. After five rings, it stopped for ten seconds then started again.

She giggled against his lips, pulling away slightly. "You can get it."

He grunted. "The day I choose that damn phone over a beautiful woman in my arms is the day you need to put me out of my misery."

She tilted her chin up, her eyes luminous as she treated him to that beautiful smile. "Maybe it's important."

The cell stopped ringing and his hotel line started. Charlie sighed and snatched it up. "Singleton."

"Great news!" Rick said. "UltimatePokerPowerhouse.net made an offer."

"I'm a little busy right now, Rick. Call me tomorrow."

"I told them to piss in the wind, of course. They totally low-balled you, but don't worry man, I'll take care of it."

"That's what I pay you for," Charlie grumbled. The offer should have been a relief, but right now, the only thing he cared about was standing in his room with too many clothes on. "Talk to you tomorrow." With that, he hung up.

"Was it urgent?" Riley asked, chewing on her bottom lip.

"To my agent, everything's urgent." He exhaled slowly and treated himself to a long head-to-toe-and-back-again look at Riley. Short black skirt, black halter, heels. Her legs were long, lithe but sculpted.

"Is he a good agent?"

Charlie groaned, grabbing her arm and tugging until her body was pressed against his. "I'm not in the mood to talk about Rick."

He pressed his lips to hers again. He'd wanted so badly to do this while they were dancing last night. She'd fit perfectly in his arms, and he'd wanted to taste her lips, to thread his fingers through her hair and kiss her until she kissed him back. He'd been fueled by more than physical attraction. He'd been fueled by sheer masculine possessiveness. He'd wanted everyone in that restaurant to know she was *his*. And this morning when he'd seen the paper, a small part of him had gloried in placing that stamp on her.

The picture of their kiss had said it all: this was Charlie Singleton's woman.

But was she?

He was loath to end their kiss, but made himself pull away. "What happened with Chaz?"

She shook her head. "I don't want him to ruin this night."

His breath left him and his shoulders relaxed as he gathered her to him. That would have to do. This night was special to her, and that was enough. For now.

He took her hand and led the way to the bedroom. When he opened the door, he saw the candles he'd lit when she arrived still burned, giving the room a soft, romantic glow.

Riley's breath hitched. "Oh."

He turned to her. "Do you like it?"

"Yes." She blinked, and her eyes were moist. "And I like you."

He ran his thumb across her cheek, over her lips. "The feeling's mutual."

Slowly, he undressed her in the candlelight. He pulled her shirt over her head then put his mouth on her collarbone, the bare curve of her shoulder, the swell of her breast, the flat of her belly. He slid her skirt from her hips and lowered himself to his knees like he had in the elevator, only this time he wouldn't be rushed. He intended to kiss every inch of her. He lifted her left foot, then her right, helping her step out of her skirt. After slipping her shoes off, he kissed each arch.

He slowly worked his way up from there, pressing his mouth against the inside of each ankle and feeling his cock swell at her stifled moan. He slid his hands up her legs, brushing his fingertips lightly between her thighs and bringing his mouth to follow the lead. When he ran his tongue along the soft flesh of her inner thighs, air left her lungs in an audible whoosh.

"Charlie," she whispered. She ran her fingers through his hair as he explored.

He looked at every inch of skin, searing it on his memory with the palm of his hands, the press of his lips, the tip of his tongue.

"You don't have to..."

He chuckled, and—an arm behind her legs, another behind her back—swept her off the floor. She yelped, and he grinned as he lowered her onto the bed.

"Sweetheart, with sex, putting on a condom is the only thing I do because I *have to*. Everything else is I do because I'm a hedonistic bastard who gets off on making you come."

He slid a hand between her legs to prove his point.

She moaned and arched her back, pressing into the pressure.

He flicked her earlobe with his tongue. "I was so hard last night, thinking about you touching yourself in your apartment. It took everything I had not to come over there and help you along."

She pulled in a ragged breath.

"You like it when I talk dirty, don't you?" He slid a finger inside her. Hell, she was so damn wet, his cock instantly grew harder.

"Your mouth is pretty vain to take credit for the work of your hands," she whispered, a smile playing at her lips as her eyes fluttered closed.

He lowered his mouth to her ear, nibbled along the shell, sucked the lobe between his teeth, all while working her with his finger. He slid a second inside her, and she took in a sharp breath.

He loved watching her face, watching how she could hardly keep her eyes open against the pleasure. "When I have my fingers inside you like this, you can't hide your reaction to my words. I feel you clench around my fingers when I talk to you. And I just bet if I tell you what's on my mind—how I want to part your legs and bury my face between them…" She pulsed around him, and he smiled. "Yeah, I was right. You like the words."

Then he did as he'd promised, sinking down on the bed and parting her legs so he could taste his fill of her.

CHAPTER
TWELVE

The elevator, the bed, the shower—Charlie still hadn't gotten his fill of her. He brushed her hair out of her face, loving the silky feel of the wet strands against his fingertips.

"Thanks for helping me overcome my fear of elevators," she whispered, a half-smile curving her lips.

"Any time you need to be distracted on an elevator ride, I'm your man."

She giggled and nuzzled her face against his chest. God, but she felt right in his arms.

"Have you always been afraid of elevators?"

Silence drew taut like a wire of energy between them. "Not always." She rolled to her back and looked at the ceiling. Her teeth tugged at her bottom lip. "I lost my mom when I was twelve."

He put his hand against her face. "Riley, I'm sorry. I had no idea." Had there been some sort of elevator accident? A fire and her mother had been trapped? "What happened?"

"Did you know she was a dancer?"

He didn't answer, didn't think she was really looking for an answer. This wasn't about him.

"She was beautiful. So talented. But she put a lot of pressure on herself to be the best in her company while also being the best mom. I knew something had changed in her, but she'd sheltered me so much I didn't have a context for understanding that she'd begun using drugs—speed, mostly, to help her get through her days. They found some downers in her purse after she died, too— probably the only way she could sleep at night."

Charlie reached down between them and grabbed her hand, threading his fingers through hers.

"We were on our way up to see my father when she died. She never took the money he'd offered her to help raise me. She was too proud. But I wanted new ballet slippers for my recital, and she couldn't afford them. She was swallowing her pride to ask him for money. I didn't know him very well then—we didn't do visitation or anything because he'd honored my mother's decision to raise me on her own. I didn't appreciate the kind of humility it took to ask my father for money. But she was doing it. Dance was so important to me. I wanted to be like her, and she could hardly afford the lessons, let alone the recital outfits."

Charlie's chest tightened. Why hadn't her father insisted on providing for Riley? Insisted on being part of her life? At least the asshole had been lucky enough to know he *had* a daughter.

"There was a big storm that day, and we were in that elevator when the power failed. Maybe it was the stress of being stuck or maybe she was anxious about seeing my father, but her heart had been battered by drug abuse, and she had a stroke. When the door opened to my father's executive suite, she was on the floor and I couldn't get her up. I screamed for help but..." She closed her eyes.

"She was already gone," Charlie finished for her.

"She was dying and I couldn't help her. For a long time I thought she wouldn't have died if we hadn't been in the elevator. I know better now. She'd been too hard on her body, and it was a matter of time." She gave a forced smile. "I guess by the time I was old enough to understand, my fear of elevators had evolved into an out-and-out phobia."

Charlie rolled so she was under him. Supporting himself on his forearms, he looked down at her. She hadn't shed a single tear telling her story, but he kissed her cheeks where the tears should have been. She closed her eyes and didn't protest, and he sank lower and kissed the skin between her breasts, right over her heart.

When he spoke, his voice was rough. "I'm so sorry," he whispered. Then he slid his arms under her, taking her with him as he rolled to his side.

She pressed her palm against his chest. "It was a long time ago."

"Hush and let me hold you," he said. He felt the moment she surrendered to it, the moment she melted against him and closed her eyes.

There was more to the story, but she didn't need to fill in the blanks for him to understand. Her father hadn't been in her life before, but he must have stepped in when her mother died. She'd lost her mother that day, but she'd also lost her life. And the new life she'd been given couldn't have been an easy one. Charlie had seen the way Riley lived to please her father. What he hadn't seen for himself, he'd heard from Lacey.

Charlie threaded his fingers through Riley's hair, wishing he could take away her hurt. Wishing he were the kind of man who stuck around...the kind women wanted to have stick around.

When he'd been served with those paternity papers, there had been a part of him that had understood Angela's decision to keep the child from him. He would be a shitty father. Or would have been. Now? He wasn't sure.

Riley moaned in her sleep and shifted to press her cheek against his chest.

I love you.

Why was it that the love of a sweet little brunette could make him believe for the first time that he could be worthy of title *father*?

He pulled Riley into his side, wanting to sleep with their bodies pressed together. The clock read 3:00. She needed to work in the morning, so he wouldn't wake her, but the smell of her skin mingled with the scent of sex on the air made him ready for her all over again.

He still couldn't believe he'd taken her in the elevator. She'd been so terrified and so vulnerable. As crazy as he would have thought it was if someone else had said so, she'd needed him to slide into her in there. She'd needed him to replace the bad memory with a good one.

Something about it still nagged at him. As if he'd exposed her. As if—

"Shit." The word came out a puff of breath against her hair, and she turned in his arms, moaning softly before settling into the soft bed again.

Carefully, so as not to wake her, Charlie shifted her and slid out of bed. He tugged on a pair of basketball shorts and trod out to the elevator. He held his breath as he waited for it to open.

The door slid open and a curse slipped from his lips as he spotted what he had wished against sense he wouldn't: surveillance cameras.

He closed his eyes. The surveillance specialists in the Grand Escape Resort and Casino surveillance room would have seen everything. Worse, they now had access to the evidence. Charlie didn't have to be a rag-mag journalist to know that footage of him and Riley going at it in the elevator would be the kind of ratings spike any network would kill for.

He didn't bother getting dressed. He headed to the surveillance room with bare feet and chest.

He pounded at the door and waited. Nothing.

The mechanisms in the camera above the door whirred as the camera swiveled to focus on him.

Shit. They weren't going to let him in for nothing. He stared straight into the camera and said, "Someone's cheating on the casino floor." Then he said a swift prayer he wasn't lying.

Sure enough, the big steel door swung open and a surveillance officer stepped out. The door closed behind him.

"Charlie Singleton." Charlie extended a hand.

The man, whose badge identified him as "Crew Chief," took Charlie's hand reluctantly. "I know who you are. What can I do for you Mr. Singleton?"

"Do you know why I'm here?"

"Not a clue," the man said, his voice dry and unamused.

"How long have you been on duty tonight?"

"My crew came on at midnight."

Charlie let out a breath. They wouldn't have been the ones behind the camera when he and Riley had been in the elevator. "I need to see some footage from around ten o'clock from the suite tower elevator."

"It's nice to want things."

"I'm willing to give you something in return."

"What's that?"

"I can show you someone who's at the casino tonight scamming you."

"My crew would have seen it."

Charlie raised a brow. "Can you be so sure? You know how bad it looks when another crew finds something your crew should have seen weeks ago."

The man studied Charlie for a long beat. "Fine. But I'm not showing you anything until you deliver."

Charlie nodded, a rush of breath leaving him as he followed the man inside. The surveillance room was filled with screens monitoring every angle of every public space in the casino.

"Where are the cameras covering the baccarat tables?" he asked.

The officer pointed to a group of screens in the corner of the room being monitored by another officer.

"There she is," Charlie said, pointing to a woman who frequented Grand Escape. Tonight the woman wore a long black dress. He'd seen her at Grand Escape enough times to guess when she'd be at the tables, and he'd watched her closely enough to know what she was doing.

"Run facial recognition software on her," the crew chief directed to his seated officer.

With a few key strokes, the woman's vital stats appeared on the screen: her name, occupation, dates she visited the casino, games she played, wins and losses, even her credit history.

Charlie let out a low whistle. "I'm impressed," he said, referring to the system.

"Not so much," the officer said, misunderstanding. "She loses more than she wins, and any wins she's had have been small."

Charlie shook his head and reached up to tap the screen that showed the woman placing a bet on another man's hand. "How's he doing?"

"We've been watching him," the crew chief said. "He's raking it in tonight, but he seems clean." He narrowed his eyes at the screen. "Search the computer for a connection between the lady in black and our man here."

"They haven't played in the same table game here before," the officer said, scanning the results as they came up on the screen. He looked up at his boss. "She used to work at the Black Diamond," he said, "and according to this the man who profited off her bets is a bouncer there."

"How'd you know they were playing the system?" the crew chief asked.

Charlie shrugged. "I noticed her the other night." Maybe it was years of playing poker, of watching for the bluff, but he had a decent eye for cheats.

The chief nodded. "I'm true to my word." He looked to the officer seated before them. "Rodney, pull up—"

"No," Charlie said. "Your eyes and mine only."

The chief gave him a knowing grin. "Oh, I get it now. Who's the special lady?"

"Like I'm going to tell you." Frankly, if Riley's identity wasn't clear from the video, he'd let it go. A sex tape of a man with a reputation wasn't the kind of news it would be if said man appeared with a woman known for her strait-laced life.

"I guess I'll see for myself soon enough," the chief said. He led Charlie to an inconspicuous corner and sat down at the keyboard. "May I ask, Mr. Singleton, what you hope to gain by seeing this footage?"

Charlie released a breath. "Right now I'm just gathering information." It all depended on whether the camera revealed Riley. If it did, well, he'd go from there.

"What time?"

"Around twenty-two hundred hours."

Suddenly the image of him walking into the elevator appeared on the screen. The time stamp on the bottom of the screen read 22:02.34. He stood in the elevator, hands in pockets as he rode down to the lobby to meet Riley. Just as the elevator doors slid open, there was a blip in the recording. The screen read 22:14.41 and Charlie was exiting the elevator behind a brunette whose face was hidden from view.

"What the hell?" The crew chief tapped at the keyboard and replayed the same sequence. He moved to another computer and repeated his keystrokes with the same results. "Holy shit," he said, looking over your shoulder. "You must have some sort of fairy godmother."

"I don't understand." Charlie narrowed his eyes at the screen.

"You'll have to come back tomorrow and talk to the guys who work the shift before ours." The crew chief stared at the screen and shook his head. "I don't know why or how, but your elevator rendezvous with the mystery woman? It's gone."

CHAPTER
THIRTEEN

Charlie woke up, his legs tangled with Riley's, his arm wrapped securely around her waist, as if he'd been afraid she'd run away in the night.

He slid his hand down her belly and between her legs and she made little moans in her sleep. She was still wet from last night, and it was easy to slip a finger inside her. He wanted her to wake up turned on, wet, and halfway to orgasm.

He swept her hair aside and nibbled down the side of her neck, tasting the sweet-salty tang of her smooth skin after a night of lovemaking.

She moaned and rolled her hips, rubbing her ass against his cock. "Charlie."

He liked the sound of his name from her sleepy lips. He could get used to waking up like this. Riley in his arms, the smell of sex in the air.

She moaned softly as he withdrew his finger. He traced its damp tip up her body, over her stomach. He found her tight nipples and rolled them softly. He was rock hard again and was thinking of sliding into her from behind when she bolted upright in bed.

She yanked the sheet to cover herself. "Oh my God!"

He grinned and tugged at it. "Nothing I haven't already seen, love."

"It's seven thirty," she said wide-eyed and slack-jawed. Her hand flew to cover her mouth. "How could I have been so careless?"

"I took the liberty of calling the concierge and sending him on a special errand for a new suit for you. It's hanging in the foyer." He ran a finger down her bare arm, resenting the hell out of the fact that she'd be leaving his bed so soon. "You won't be late."

She pushed herself off the bed, studying the floor. "I don't even want to know where he bought a suit in the hours I was asleep," she muttered.

"You of all people should know a Grand Escape VIP need only ask to see his wish granted."

Last night, after he'd taken her on the bed, he'd led her to the shower. Her dark hair had been wet when they'd fallen back into bed, sated and exhausted, and now it fell in ringlets around her face as she paced. "I like your hair like that. Why do you straighten it?"

"I must look like an ungroomed poodle." Her hands slipped into her hair as she searched the floor.

"It you're looking for your panties, you needn't bother. I took care of everything." He motioned his head toward the other room. "See for yourself."

She frowned and left him without a word.

"You're welcome," he muttered, pulling himself out of bed to follow her. Since she clearly wasn't in the mood for naked—damn shame—he tugged on some jeans.

She was already in the bra and panties when he joined her, but something had stopped her progress. She stood frozen by the desk. "What is this?"

Charlie took a breath. There was no use trying to hide what she could see with her own eyes. "It's a subpoena for paternity testing."

Finally pulling her eyes off the papers, she looked up at him. The hurt in her eyes was a punch in the gut.

"I have to go." She grabbed the skirt off the hanger and slid into it.

"Can I ask why the rush?" He cast a glance at the clock. "You don't work until nine and your office is just over in the other tower."

"We have a seven o'clock breakfast meeting this morning," she said, her fingers shaking at the buttons on her blouse. "An important meeting."

"So you overslept. It happens to the best of us, Ry. It's not the end of the world."

"It doesn't happen to me. My father…" She shook her head. "You wouldn't understand."

Charlie flinched. "No. I guess I wouldn't."

She brushed her hair back with her fingers, pulling the curls straight and yanking it into a tight twist at the back of her head. "My purse?"

He picked it up off the table and handed it to her.

She pulled a clip out of the front pocket and slid it in her hair. Hidden were the soft and sultry curls, gone was the wildly sensual woman who'd looked at him across the elevator threshold and asked for his help to conquer her fears.

She pulled on the suit jacket as she walked to the door, and he didn't bother following.

Only as she stood in the open doorway did she turn back to him. "I'm sorry to run out like this, and thanks. For the suit and everything."

So that was it. She was just going to sum last night up to *and everything*.

She slid out before he could find his voice to respond.

"Anytime," he whispered against the *click* of the closing door.

Across the room, he spotted the skirt and top she'd worn last night. He padded over to it and picked it up. He pressed it to his nose. Jesus, he loved the smell of her.

He didn't want to keep her this morning, but he would explain about the papers. He'd explain that he'd never been told about his son. He'd never been given the chance to do the right thing.

It had spooked her. He'd seen it in her eyes, but she didn't know the whole story. And he didn't plan on letting her run away without listening.

Riley didn't know whom she was playing with if she thought Charlie Singleton would fold that easily.

...

RILEY STOOD frozen outside of Charlie's suite. Her body was frozen but chaos reigned inside her. She stared at the elevator and the gleaming doors stared right back at her. Her pulse quickened and her stomach pitched.

He has a child.

Words played on repeat in her mind, like a scratched record: *paternity testing.* Part of him had wanted him to deny it, but he'd been so matter-of-fact. As if this was just part of being Charlie "the Devil" Singleton.

Another part of her was panicked at the possibility of what would have happened if she hadn't seen those papers.

Charlie was amazing. The way he'd fed her at dinner. His text messages after. The way he'd helped her overcome her fears and step into an elevator twice in as many nights. The way he'd touched her and tasted her.

Charlie was a man who made a girl feel like she was the only thing that mattered, and it would have been easy to leave his room this morning believing their affair could turn into something... more.

She fought the urge to turn back and tell him to explain away the papers. The man could so easily turn into an addiction she didn't have control over. Then what would happen when she wanted more and he couldn't give it?

"Let this be a lesson to you," she mumbled to herself. Her father may not have been in her life before her mother died, but no one had needed to draw up court papers to get him to step up to his responsibilities. He'd taken her in without question, and before she'd even settled into her new life, he'd given her his last name. Those papers were proof that Charlie wouldn't do the same.

She pushed those thoughts aside. She had to get to work, and the elevator was her only viable option.

She could do this. She'd done it twice now, hadn't she? Sure, once the elevator had been glass and really not that scary, and the second time Charlie had been…distracting her, but if she'd done it *twice*, she could do it again.

Palms sweating, she lunged forward to press the button before she could talk herself out of it.

The arrows above the elevator lit up, and she held her breath. When the doors opened, she could run inside, press the button for the lobby and just close her eyes until she got there. She could do this.

The doors opened and she rushed inside. Her heart pounded. Illogically, she wondered how she was supposed to face her greatest fear when the most amazing man she'd ever been with had turned out to be exactly the kind of man she needed to steer clear of.

"Shit." She shot a hand out and stopped the doors from closing. When they slid back open, she hurried back into the hall. She fumbled in her purse for her phone. It was already a quarter to eight, and her father's retirement breakfast would be half over by now.

She pressed two on her speed dial and prayed Lacey had her phone on her today.

She only had to wait through two long, torturous rings before Lacey picked up.

"Good morning, sunshine," Lacey greeted, her voice singsong sweet. "Where did you sleep last night?"

Riley looked at the ceiling and swallowed. "I don't have time to go into it right now. Are you near the front desk?"

"Yes, ma'am."

"I'm in the penthouse tower, and I can't take the elevator."

Lacey squealed. "You're *where*? What are you doing up there? Wait. Isn't that where my brother is staying?"

"Lace, I'm in a hurry, and I need to take the stairs."

"Oh." Lacey's voice grew serious. "I see," she said.

Riley chewed on her lip. "Do you?"

"The best I can do is shut the alarm off the second it sounds."

Riley closed her eyes. *Stupid, stupid, stupid.* This was her fault. Had she forgotten last night that what goes up must come down?

"You're going to get complaints," she said.

"I have a few leftover vouchers for free drinks in the bar. I can handle complaints."

"Okay. I'm heading that way in about ten seconds."

"Got ya covered, sister."

"Thanks, Lace."

She ended the call and turned to the stairwell. The closed door had a large sign: EMERGENCY EXIT ONLY. ALARM WILL SOUND.

Riley counted backward from ten and pushed through, wincing when the fire alarm blared overhead. In less than two seconds, the alarm was silenced, but she knew the shrill sound was loud enough to wake any hotel guest who'd been sleeping in—and since this was a hotel/casino, there was a large number of them.

She rushed down the stairs, and pressed through another set of marked doors when she reached the lobby. Again, the alarm sounded, and again was silenced almost immediately.

After darting across the lobby, she tugged off her shoes and sprinted up the stairs in the business tower. Perspiration beaded on her brow and at the back of her neck by the time she reached the executive level.

She straightened her suit as she scurried toward her father's boardroom, and tried not to think too much about how angry he would be when she walked in almost a full hour late.

His was the first face to greet her as she slipped in the side door. "Riley. I was wondering if you were going to join us today." Her father's voice tried at playful, but his disapproval hardened his eyes.

People were milling around, the remnants of a concluded meeting.

Riley forced a smile. "I'm sorry I'm late."

He gave a curt nod and turned back to Chaz, who extended his hand and smiled like the cat happily digesting the canary. "Congratulations on your retirement, sir. I will see you this evening."

Her father shot a hard look at Riley and retreated to his office.

Her stomach clenched as the door shut behind him.

"Riley," Chaz said softly.

She took her attention off her departing father and gave it to Chaz. "Yes?" She wasn't sure how she should feel after last night. Angry? Hurt? Bitter? One of those would make sense, but none came to the surface as she looked at his face, took in his furrowed brow. Instead, she only felt a hollow grief for the life they might have had together, the life she had imagined for years.

"Listen, about last night—"

She shook her head. "You don't owe me any explanation." Each word that came from her mouth lifted a weight from her shoulders. "You're right. I turned you down when you proposed. I think—"

He crossed the space between them and put a finger to her lips, silencing her. His skin was cold, clammy, a striking contrast to Charlie's heat. "What you saw last night…I was ending a flirtation. I wanted to start fresh." He smiled. "With you."

She stepped back and his hand dropped between them. "I don't want that anymore," she whispered.

Chaz frowned. "I don't expect you to know what you want, not after last night." He took her hand, toyed with her fingers. "Remember when we used to talk about the future? What it would be like to be married? To make a home?"

She closed her eyes against the warmth the idea brought her. How could she be but minutes out of Charlie's bed and stand here wanting what another man offered? But was it Chaz that appealed to her or the idea of having her own family?

"Remember when we used to talk about being each other's family?" He tipped her chin up and she looked into his eyes. "About making babies?"

She bit the inside of her cheek to stop the tears that threatened to fill her eyes. She wanted all those things. But she no longer wanted them with Chaz.

You want them with Charlie, a little voice whispered in her mind. Not only was that ridiculous—they'd only spent a single night together—it was impossible. Charlie couldn't give her that life. He was the kind of man who had to be summoned to lay claim to his own children.

Riley opened her mouth, still not sure what to say. This time

Chaz stopped her with his mouth, brushing it softly against hers.

She didn't kiss him back but didn't stop him either. His kisses had never lit her on fire, but they'd always been comforting. Now, even that was gone.

He pulled away and smiled. "Go to dinner with me tonight?"

"Tonight's dance class."

"So skip it." He squeezed her fingertips. "For me."

"You can come by the apartment tomorrow evening," she said, her own words muffling the warning bells at the back of her mind. Regardless of where this went, they needed to talk. She needed to give him his ring back. To end things officially.

"It's a deal." He gave her a soft smile and tapped her temple with his index finger. "Just don't ruin things by analyzing everything between now and then."

She sighed. "Chaz, you just told me not to think."

He cocked his head and studied her for a beat. "You're changing, Riley." And with that he left her office.

Riley didn't waste any time before sitting at her desk and getting to work. Maybe she was changing, but she wasn't sure it was so bad. She'd had wine in the middle of the week. Not bad. She'd danced with a notorious bad boy in the middle of the Eiffel Tower Restaurant. The media lash back had been unwanted but not terrible. She'd been so brazen as to have sex in an elevator.

Her hands froze on her keyboard. The elevator.

Grand Escape had excellent security, including cameras and surveillance in every elevator. Which meant that last night when Charlie had taken her up against the elevator wall, they'd had an audience.

She pressed in intercom and waited for her father's response. "Yes?"

She licked her lips nervously. "Daddy, I need to run out for a minute. Can I pick you up a latte while I'm gone?"

"Sure, that'd be great." He paused for a beat. "Riley, is everything okay? Is there anything you want to tell me?"

"No." She worried her lip between her teeth. "Everything's just fine, Daddy."

CHAPTER
FOURTEEN

"You're here."

Charlie dropped his arms and backed away from the heavy bag at the sound of the kid's voice. He wiped the sweat off his forehead. "I said I would be."

Derrick narrowed his eyes. "You don't have a reputation for being the most reliable guy."

"Do you believe everything you hear on the idiot box?"

Derrick grinned and a dimple appeared. The sight of it almost knocked Charlie over.

"Here," Charlie said, moving to hold the bag. "I need a break. You go first today."

For fifteen minutes, they didn't speak. The only sounds that filled the room were the thumps of the kid's fists against the bag and his low grunts when he hit hard.

When Derrick came off the bag, he bent over, hands on thighs, breathing hard. "I know why you were so pissed yesterday."

"You do, huh?"

Derrick looked up and grinned. "I was right. It was a woman. That sucks that she's marrying someone else."

Charlie threw a couple of punches at the bag before tossing a glance at the kid. "What do you know about it?"

He shrugged. "Just what was in the paper this morning."

Charlie froze in mid-punch, thinking of the missing elevator footage. He swung around. "What was in the paper?" Fuck. He hadn't even looked at the paper this morning.

"Whoa!" The kid lifted his hands, showing his palms. "Don't hurt the messenger."

Charlie took a step forward. "Just tell me what you saw."

"Just an article about that hotel heiress. There was a picture of her fiancé down on one knee and another of you kissing her." Derrick narrowed his eyes. "You're really hung up on her, aren't you?"

Charlie pulled a hand through his hair, closing his eyes for a minute as his heart painfully resumed its beating. "You could say that," he said, swallowing.

"Did you take my advice? Did you tell her how you feel?" His innocent eyes looked hopeful.

Charlie wished he could tell him life really was that simple. That if you had the balls to confess your feelings to the girl who was way out of your league, then you got to keep her. "She's not going to marry him," he grumbled.

The kid grinned. "Then the paper got it wrong? She picked you?"

His mind filled with the image of Riley's face when she saw the subpoena—hurt, stricken, like he'd taken a ball bat to her hopes and dreams. "I don't think she's picked anyone. I'm not exactly the kind of guy her father would approve of."

The kid grinned. "I wouldn't have thought you were the kind of guy who needed his approval."

Charlie couldn't help but laugh. "You're pretty smart, kid."

The smile fell from Derrick's face and he broke eye contact. "If things work out between you and the hotel heiress, would you move back to Vegas?"

Charlie frowned. What did the kid want from him? "I haven't gotten that far yet," he confessed.

The kid nodded but stepped forward to hit on the bag rather than look at Charlie. "Must be pretty cool to live in LA, huh? You're lucky your mom let you leave."

Charlie hadn't given her the choice, but he'd been too young and dumb to care that he was breaking his mother's heart when he dropped out of school to head to LA. Charlie's phone beeped from his gym bag, saving him from responding. He squatted to pull his cell from his bag, and found a message from Riley. *We need to talk. Can you come to my office?*

Usually when women said those words after a night of sex, Charlie wanted to run in the other direction. Getting them from Riley just made him smile.

"That from her?" Derrick asked, hovering over Charlie's shoulder.

"Yeah. It is."

He turned, and the kid was grinning. "Well, don't leave her hanging, man."

Charlie returned the smile. "You're all right, kid." He hitched his gym bag over his shoulder and was two steps to the door before Derrick stopped him.

"You gonna be here tomorrow?"

Charlie froze. He'd never had a father to teach him how to do this. He'd never learned what it meant to be a dad. He turned back to Derrick. "I'll be playing poker with some friends in here on Sunday."

The kid's face fell. "Oh. Okay."

"Why don't you come?"

He grinned. "You'll teach me?"

"You don't know how to play Texas Hold 'Em?"

"I know how to play. I want you to teach me how to win."

Charlie grinned. "I can do that." Hell, but he could really like this kid.

...

"How did you do it?"

Riley paced her office, arms wrapped around herself. Everyone had cleared out for the day, and Riley had waited here until Charlie arrived. She had no idea how he would have convinced someone to erase that footage. When she'd gone down to the surveillance room, she'd done so knowing that even *she* wouldn't have been able to talk her surveillance officers into erasing it. Grand Escape took security very seriously. Gaps in footage meant a pink slip for whoever had access to the server.

"How did I do what?" he asked.

She forced her feet to still and put her hands on her hips. "How did you erase the footage from the elevator? No one has access to those servers and my father's staff is beyond reproach." She swallowed, not wanting to say the rest. "And if anyone did let you tamper with the footage…he needs to be let go."

Charlie raised a brow, and Riley put her palm out to stop him. "Listen, I'm the last person who wants there to be evidence of our… mistake…but I have the security of Grand Escape to consider."

"I agree."

Her shoulders sagged, though she wasn't sure why that meant so much to her.

"I would have told you what I know this morning, but you seemed a little…"

She winced. "I'm sorry about that."

"While you were sleeping, I remembered our *mistake*, as you call it." His icy blue eyes burned into hers. "And for the record, the only part that was a mistake was the location."

Riley swallowed. She wasn't sure she agreed, but even now she felt that draw to him. Sexually speaking, the man had the gravitational pull of the sun.

"When I went down to the surveillance room, I was able to talk one of the guys into seeing the footage. It was three in the morning and a new shift had just come on. They were as shocked as I was to see the footage was gone."

She blinked and staggered back. "What?"

"All that is on the server is you and me walking onto the elevator. Then there's a fifteen-minute gap and we're walking out."

Riley knew from experience that if something seemed too good to be true, it probably was. "How could that be?"

Charlie ran a hand through his dark hair. "Hell if I know."

"Charlie, if you're trying to protect someone, stop. I know you wouldn't want whoever helped you to lose their job, but I need to—"

"I'm telling the truth, Riley." His words were soft but this frustration seeped through.

Her mind spun through possibilities, but nothing stuck.

"Do you think one of your guys could have alerted your father to what he'd seen?" He rubbed the back of his neck. "Maybe trying to protect you?"

Riley closed her eyes. Her stomach pitched at the possibility of her father being pulled out of bed to see that footage. He would have taken care of it. She didn't doubt it. "That's the most logical explanation." And it explained why he'd been so awkward with her this morning.

Charlie pulled her into his arms, and Riley let him. Sure, he was the kind of man who made a girl do something stupid like have elevator sex. He was the kind of man who might have children he didn't even know about. He was the kind of man she needed to stay far away from, but right now his heat comforted her in a way she desperately needed.

She looked up at him and focused on his mouth. God, that mouth had done things to her last night—wicked, delicious things. She'd told herself she was done with him. Playing with Charlie Singleton was playing with fire, and she couldn't afford any more scars.

But he was here now and she couldn't deny herself one more taste of him.

"We should talk about the papers you saw this morning," he said softly.

She drew her bottom lip between her teeth and made a decision. "No. We shouldn't."

"Riley—"

She put up a hand. "Charlie, you don't owe me any explanation. This—" She wanted to tell him their relationship wasn't like that, but it was too embarrassing to admit out loud that she had considered—even for a moment—the possibility of something real, something long term and exclusive with a man like Charlie.

She couldn't bring herself to say the words. Instead, she decided to explain with her mouth. She lifted onto her toes and pressed her lips against his, hoping he would understand.

He pulled away for a moment, studying her through dark, thick lashes. Then he lowered his mouth to hers, his touch soft, his movements tentative. She plunged her hands into his hair and his kiss grew stronger, bolder, more demanding. It was a messy kiss. Tongues slid against each other, teeth nipped at lips, hands grasped for bare flesh.

They both came away breathing heavily.

He brushed his thumb across her cheek. "I have to go."

"Where—" She stopped herself. He didn't need to report his whereabouts to her.

He answered anyway. "To the surveillance room. The crew should be on now that was on shift during our...elevator ride."

She nodded. "Right. I'll go with you."

"No. There's a chance that your face isn't clear on the tapes. Until we know otherwise, I'm keeping you out of this."

She opened her mouth to protest and then thought it through. He was right. A sex tape of Charlie and a random woman wouldn't be news...not unless they knew it was her. "Okay. Send me a text and let me know what you find out."

Charlie smirked. "As if I'd pass up an opportunity to engage those fingers."

...

MARTIN GRIMINSKI was the second shift surveillance crew chief, and Charlie didn't have to say a word to get a conference with the man. He came out of the surveillance room, his round belly shaking with silent chuckles. In a red shirt that strained at the buttons, the man looked a little like Santa Claus but with a shorter beard.

"If it isn't the Devil," he said, smacking Charlie on between the shoulder blades. "I heard you visited third-shift boys last night, and I think I know why."

Charlie felt his cheeks heat despite himself. He was far from modest, but this was too much. "What happened to the footage?" he asked, forcing himself to move past his embarrassment.

Griminski glanced into the control room a final time before closing the door. "Let's go for a walk," he said.

Charlie followed as Griminski led him out of Grand Escape and to a coffee shop a few doors down.

They were seated at a table before Griminski spoke again. "I've worked for Quinton Carter for a lot of years."

Charlie sighed. "Listen, if you're trying to establish what a lucky bastard I am that you're talking to me at all, I already know. You don't have to prove it."

Griminski chuckled. "We both know that Carter's concern in this has little to do with the fact that he's my boss."

Charlie winced. Riley's face had shown on the recording then.

"Did you know that Mr. Carter had another daughter?"

Charlie raised a brow. "Riley has a sister?"

Griminski lifted his palms. "Sure, if you want to look at it that way, but they weren't raised together. His other daughter was, oh, about twenty, twenty-two years older than Riley. In fact, she was dead before Carter ever adopted Riley."

"Dead?"

Griminski nodded. "Murdered."

"Jesus. I had no idea."

"Yeah, well, it was only a news item at the time because of who her father was. She was trouble, that girl. Ran with the wrong crowds, was mixed up in drugs and the sex industry. Sounds bad to say it, but those of us who knew how she lived weren't surprised. She was at the wrong place at the wrong time."

"Carter must have been torn up." Charlie shook his head. "I don't mean to sound like an ass, but I'm not following. What does this have to do with the missing video footage?"

"I worked for Carter back when his daughter Chelsea was running around. He couldn't control her, and after trying only pushed her further away—he did what he could for damage control. And where did he have more control than his own casino?

"The rule was, if we had footage of his daughter doing

something morally, legally, or ethically…questionable, the footage was pulled from the rest of the tapes and given to Carter."

"So this procedure continued when Riley came along?"

Griminski shrugged his broad shoulders. "I don't really know. It's never been an issue. Riley isn't the free spirit her sister was. But when I saw her get on that elevator with you, I figured better to follow the old procedure and let the old man know I had the footage if he wanted it. I burned the DVD and deleted the footage from the hard drive."

"So her father has it now?"

Griminski looked at his watch. "Nope, I left him a voicemail and am still waiting to hear back."

"I don't suppose I could talk you into handing it over to me? I have a checking account that can be pretty convincing."

"And risk my neck when Carter finds out there's unaccounted-for missing footage from last night? Hell no. Dude, don't worry. I'll let him know the gist of the contents and he won't have anything to do with it."

Charlie let out a hard breath. It wasn't ideal, but it would have to do. "Thanks for your time, man. I know you didn't have to."

"You're right. I didn't, but I figure we owe you for the way you helped us catch that woman last night. You really didn't know her?"

Charlie shrugged. "No, I just have an eye for that kind of thing."

"Huh. Well, if you ever leave poker, you might consider a job as a surveillance specialist. We can always use guys with eyes like yours."

He waved away the suggestion. "Appreciate you thinking of me, but I don't even have my high school diploma." It wasn't something he liked to talk about, but it was the truth. "I know your guys have minimum of two-year degrees."

Griminski leaned forward, studying him. "Don't rule it out."

CHAPTER
FIFTEEN

Riley had decided to treat herself to an evening in her PJs. Her acrobatic penguin nightgown and the company of Jaws, who lay on the couch gnawing on a new rawhide, were the least she deserved after the week she'd had.

Her cell buzzed with a new text. The screen notification reminded her there was someone else she needed to clear the air with.

"Lace, we need to talk."

Lacey looked up from her *People* magazine and frowned. "Okay. What's up?"

Riley took the magazine from her friend, placing it on the end table.

Lacey's eyebrows shot up. "Wowza. Important stuff."

"I just got a text message," Riley said, holding up her phone. Among other things she'd failed to do in the last twelve hours was fix the programming mix-up on her phone. To illustrate her point, she positioned her phone so Lacey could see the screen that read: *Text Message from Charles Spencer.*

Lacey's face said it all. Her eyes grew wide; her jaw dropped an inch.

Riley sighed. "So it *was* intentional."

Her friend pulled her bottom lip between her teeth. "What happened?"

Riley leaned back on the couch and looked at the ceiling. "Some text messages. Real harmless stuff at first, but I thought it was Chaz..." She swallowed, letting Lacey draw her own conclusions.

"Ry, listen. It was impulsive. I was programming your phone and their numbers are right there next to each other in your address book: Charles Singleton and Charles Spencer. At first, it was a mistake. I just swapped the numbers. When I realized what I'd done, I immediately went to fix it, and then..." She looked at her hands. "I decided not to fix it."

"And proceeded to suggest I send *Chaz* dirty text messages."

Lacey winced. "It was stupid. Dishonest. But I hate seeing you with someone who doesn't make you happy."

Riley tugged at her ponytail. "You can't just mess with my life."

Lacey huffed. "Do you have any idea what it's like to live with you? I see you spend every day trying to be this perfect daughter. You sacrifice everything to get your father's approval, and what kind of life is that?"

Riley bolted to standing. "It's *my* life."

Lowering her head, Lacey frowned. "I love you too much to keep being silent. You have life and passion inside you. Why keep it bottled away?"

Riley couldn't be mad at her friend. Not after what she'd seen at Chaz's place last night. Would she have ever have learned the truth if Lacey hadn't switched their numbers? Likely she would have, but when? After another two years of him leading her to believe their relationship was going somewhere? Would she have learned the truth after five years of marriage?

"Listen, I didn't mean to push you on my brother. I mean, he's sweet on you, but he might not be The One. I don't want you to think—"

She stopped when Riley huffed. "I don't think Charlie 'the Devil' Singleton is The One for anyone, Lace. Finding The One is like finding the perfect cup of coffee. Charlie's more like a mimosa—a treat, an indulgence, but nothing you should plan on waking up to every morning."

Lacey frowned.

"What?" Riley smiled. "That's who your brother is, and—last I checked—he's damn proud of it."

"Maybe he just hasn't found the right girl yet."

Riley waved away Lacey's protest. Lace probably liked to imagine her brother would eventually settle down, get married, have a couple kids.

Still frowning, Lacey sat back in her chair. "So, are you dating him?"

"Not *dating*." Riley wasn't sure what she would call what she and Charlie were doing. In fact, she wasn't sure there was a name for it aside from *having hot sex in inappropriate places*.

"But you broke up with Chaz?"

Riley nodded. "More or less."

Lacey mumbled something, and Riley thought she might have said, *Well, that's good, at least.*

She took a breath, pushing aside the temptation to ask Lacey about Charlie's paternity suit. If Riley wanted to know more—and she didn't—she needed to go to Charlie, not his sister.

"I'm really sorry, Riley," Lacey whispered. "It was stupid and I hope you'll forgive me."

Riley exhaled sharply and nodded. "Of course I do. But Lacey, that's it, okay? No more running interference between me and the life I choose to live."

Lacey chewed her lip. "Fair." She nodded to Riley's phone. "You going to answer that or do you plan to keep my brother waiting?"

Riley smiled and opened the text.

I can't stop thinking about you.

The second her eyes ran over the words, she wanted him. Wanted to hear his voice, smell his scent, feel his hands on her. She licked her lips. Could she do this? Could she carry on with a man with whom there was no possibility of a future? Could she have a true affair just for the pleasure of it?

*So, tell me more about these thoughts…*she wrote, taking a self-conscious peek at Lacey from the corner of her eye.

You, that bustier I bought you, and leather handcuffs. And that's just the beginning.

She smiled. Yes, she could. Charlie would keep her on track. He'd remind her what this relationship was really about. She bit her lip as she typed her reply. Three sentences, two texts, and he had arousal turning slow circles low in her belly. *You keep mentioning these handcuffs, but I'm not sure I believe they exist.*

Careful, Riley. That sounded like a dare.

Maybe it was.

The silent seconds as she waited for his response were filled with the sensation of her nipples tightening and blood rushing between her legs.

So fucking tempting. But not tonight.

Are you buying some other woman lingerie tonight? she typed. She meant to be teasing, but she realized there was a part of her that hated the idea of him with another woman.

You got part of it right. Have you found the package yet?

Riley frowned. *What package?*

I left it on your pillow.

Standing, Riley looked to Lacey. "Was Charlie here earlier?"

Lacey nodded. "Yeah, he visited a little while you were at dance class."

Riley shot to her bedroom, smiling as she wondered what Charlie had left her.

The Fredrick's box sat on her pillow, a skinny ribbon across its middle. Riley fought her schoolgirl grin as she lowered herself onto the mattress. She positioned the box in her lap.

After casting a quick glance over her shoulder to make sure Lacey hadn't followed her into the bedroom, she slid the ribbon off the end and lifted the lid. There wasn't much inside, but the little that was there made her insides flip-flop.

Black lace panties with ties at each hip, and a barely there black lace bra that had so little fabric, she wasn't even sure it qualified as demi-cup.

But what really sent her belly a buzz was the note in Charlie's solid hand: *I'll be by at seven. Wear whatever you want on top and these underneath. Tonight, I show you what's it's like to do Vegas with the Devil.*

She pulled her lip between her teeth and clenched her thighs together. How could he send her this and then tell her they'd spend their evening in public? Didn't he know that this gift would make her want to be alone with him?

Her phone beeped. *Will you be ready?*

Yes.

She took a breath. She was an adult who'd had twenty-six years of practice in self-restraint. She could do this. Her only real problem was she had no idea what to wear. She hadn't spent much time in the casinos—she preferred managing the controlled chaos to experiencing it—but she knew enough to know that not a single item in her closet was appropriate for the kind of night Charlie had in mind.

She glanced at the clock. Six p.m. She didn't have enough time to go shopping. There was only one solution.

"Lacey!"

Lacey stuck her head in Riley's door. "Yes?"

"I need an outfit for a night on the town," she said. "Can you help?"

Lacey's lips curved into a cat-who-ate-the-canary grin, and she pressed her door open all the way and gestured inside. "This is going to be fun."

...

THERE WAS only one thing in this world that Charlie enjoyed more than a beautiful woman: a woman who had made herself beautiful for him. And the only thing that could top *that* was *Riley* making herself up just for him.

She wore a red gown in some filmy fabric that draped over her curves and stopped just below her knees. Red-painted toes peeked out of strappy red sandals. Her hair was down in waves around her shoulders, a lock swept back from her face in sparkling clip, exposing glittering rubies at her ears. Her eyes were lined, and her lips were painted to match her dress.

At the sight of her, his stomach clenched with some emotion he couldn't identify—or wasn't sure he wanted to.

He ran his gaze over her again—bare toes to bare shoulders to wide eyes—and thought that he had to be the luckiest fucking bastard on the planet.

"I don't normally dress like this," she explained.

He raised a brow. "Damn shame."

Her lip twitched, a smile pulling at it. "Your sister helped."

He extended his hand for hers, and as she put her small fingers into his palm, he said, "Remind me to buy her something really expensive to express my gratitude." In one quick movement, he pulled her to him and pressed his lips to hers.

She responded instantly, opening her mouth beneath him and sliding a hand inside his jacket.

He wrapped an arm around her, pulling her close so he could feel all those curves pressed against him. Knowing what she wore underneath only added to the sweet torture.

"A-hem!"

Charlie broke the kiss, and looked over Riley's head to see Lacey standing behind her, hands on hips. "Can I count on you to have her home by midnight?"

Charlie swallowed, his mind still swimming from the effects of Riley's kiss. At the moment, he wasn't interested in taking her anywhere but her bedroom. He'd resist that urge. He was here to woo her. Sex could wait.

Riley turned to her friend, leaning back against Charlie's chest. "Midnight is unlikely, Lace."

Lacey frowned. "Well, I won't be at work in the morning to shut off the fire alarm, so you better bring her home instead of taking her up to that suite of yours."

Charlie looked down at Riley, questioning. Riley shook her head.

Lacey crossed her arms over her chest and looked them up and down. "You two look good together."

"Then why do you look so worried?" Riley asked.

"Because I can't decide which one of you is more likely to get hurt."

Riley waved a hand, dismissing her concern. "See you later, Lacey. Don't wait up." She laced her fingers with Charlie's and led him into the hall.

Charlie pulled the door shut after them. "Wait," he said softly as Riley started to head to the stairs.

She turned, looking up at him.

His breath caught. Would he ever get over how beautiful she was? Tracing his thumb along the edge of her jaw, he said, "You know I won't hurt you, right?"

She wrinkled her nose, still smiling. "Said the lion to the gazelle."

"No, I—" He dipped his head, kissing her softly. When he pulled away, her eyes were closed, and she touched her tongue to her bottom lip, as if looking for his taste there. "I won't hurt you," he repeated.

Her eyes fluttered open and she shook her head. "I may be relatively inexperienced, Charlie, but I'm not naïve. I know what this is. Don't worry about me."

She headed for the stairs and Charlie frowned. What did she mean by that?

CHAPTER
SIXTEEN

"So, where are we going? Didn't we do the romantic dinner thing a couple nights ago?" Not that she minded. She'd had too few romantic dinners for a twenty-six-year-old woman. Chaz had taken her out, but it had never felt like wooing. And he'd *never* picked her up in a limo. Not unless her father had somehow footed the bill.

Charlie leaned forward and opened the mini-fridge. He studied its contents for a moment before choosing a bottle. "Last time," he explained, "you belonged to someone else. Tonight, you're mine." He turned the bottle to her. "Champagne?"

Riley nodded. "Please." She bit her lip. "What makes you think I'm yours now?"

Charlie popped the cork on the champagne and poured her a glass. "Well," he said, offering the golden liquid to her, "are you *his*?"

As she took the glass from him, their fingers brushed, and for a moment the air between them thickened with awareness, lust, and primitive need. "I'm not his," she said, shaking her head to clear the fog, and thinking, *I'm not anyone's*. "Let's not talk about Chaz. Tonight isn't about him."

"No, tonight's about letting go, cutting loose." He raised his glass. "To fun."

She clinked her glass to his. "Your specialty."

He winked at her as he took a sip of his champagne, and she followed his lead, pouring the bubbly liquid on her tongue.

Riley had indulged in champagne on five other occasions in her life. Four times belonged to the midnight on each New Year's Eve since she'd turned twenty-one. The other time, she'd been sixteen and snuck a boy into her house. Charlie Singleton reminded her all too much of Adam Renard, the tall, dark, and handsome jock from the wrong side of the tracks. Adam had talked her out of the key to her father's wine cellar then, later, her virginity.

She smiled into her champagne. Usually, she was ashamed to remember those days—a precious few weeks of rebellious youth when she'd dared to live a life that pleased her more than it pleased her father. In a couple months' time, Adam had introduced her to her ING, and then Riley and her hidden naughty side had been fast friends.

Once—in a rush of defiant independence—Riley had even told her father to *fuck off.* Oh, he'd been angry. But more than that, he'd been shocked. When she'd moved in with him at twelve years of age, he'd taken the reins of her life into both of his hands and carefully guided *every* move she'd made. Imagine his surprise when he came home to find his daughter, the girl the media had already labeled Vegas' Good Daughter, drunk on his expensive champagne and naked in the arms of some kid who did not meet his list of requirements.

Sometimes she'd wondered how her life would have been different if Adam hadn't been as terrified of Quinton Carter as the rest of the world was. She couldn't blame him. He'd been a kid at the time, and in addition to a daunting physique, her father had considerable social and political power. When he'd threatened to destroy Adam's future, Adam had been right to believe him.

When she'd sobered up—alone—she'd come to her senses, and her father had found her a nice girls' school where she could finish her high school education.

"What are you smiling about?" Charlie asked. He sat across

from her in the limo, his long legs extended in front of him, crossed at the ankle. Broad shoulders, narrow hips, hard body, he filled his dark suit perfectly—so perfectly that when he'd shown up at her door she'd found herself wondering how well he would fit into the corporate world. She'd had to shake away the thought—that was a mind used to measuring up men as potential spouses, and she wasn't interested in Charlie's spouse-potential. This was about something else. He'd nailed it perfectly with their toast: *fun.*

"The champagne reminds me of my wild youth," she admitted, answering his question.

Charlie raised a disbelieving brow. "Oh? Do tell."

She shrugged. She didn't want to tell him of a time when she'd been brave enough to think, do, and act for herself. How could she confess she'd only known what that was like for a few months when he'd been living that life for as long as he could remember? "It was short-lived. I'm just glad it lived at all. Every girl needs a few wild memories."

He leaned forward, settling his elbows on his knees. "You're still young," he said softly, his eyes locked on hers. "Who says you can't make more?"

She grinned. "Is that an invitation?"

Charlie shrugged carelessly, and she threw back the rest of her champagne. Charlie leaned across his seat and flipped a switch, and sultry club music filled the limo.

She crossed to him, and before she could hesitate, she hiked her dress and straddled his hips.

Charlie groaned, a deep, rumbling sound in the back of his throat. She lowered her mouth to his, anxious to be swept away by the high created by his touch. If Charlie Singleton was a drug, she was a helpless addict.

As his tongue slid into her mouth, she circled her hips, rubbing against his erection.

Charlie's arms snaked around her, his hands grasping her ass and pulling her more tightly against him.

He was right, of course. She was still young. Young and as free as she'd ever been. If she disappointed her father, so what? Was he going to give the job she'd worked and trained for to someone else? He'd already done that. What could he do now?

She slid her hands inside Charlie's jacket, wanting to feel the heat and strength of the muscles under his shirt, wanting his physical strength to carry over into her, to give her the emotional strength she needed to venture out on her own.

Charlie's mouth left hers as he trailed kisses along her jaw, over her collarbone, up her neck. "Are you wearing the panties I sent you?" The question was whispered in her ear.

She nodded, licking her lips as sensations from his tongue against her earlobe whipped through her.

"You know what I love about them?" he asked, his breath hot against her ear.

"What?" her voice was scratchy, rough against her sudden need.

"With the ties at the hips"—he slid a hand up her skirt and toyed with the ties that lay against one hipbone—"I could just untie your panties right here in the limo. You can straddle me like this, and we can ride around Vegas, watching the lights while I come inside you."

She wasn't sure what it said about her that the idea held so much appeal. "What are you waiting for?"

He ran a thumb over her lips, and she sucked it into her mouth. He closed his eyes and his cock pulsed to life between her legs.

"Tonight isn't about sex."

Riley laughed, sliding her hand between their bodies to stroke his erection. He let out a low hiss.

Just the feel of his erection through his pants and she burned to feel him inside her again. *He* did this to her. She'd never been like this before. Not with anyone. "I bet I could change your mind."

She backed up carefully, until she was on her knees before him. "Riley—"

She put her finger to his lips. "Is tonight for me?"

"Absolutely," he said softly.

"And I can have whatever fun I want?" she asked, her hands already at his zipper.

"You don't have to—" His eyes closed as she squeezed his now-bare cock in her hand.

"I want to."

Before he could protest, she licked the tip of him, loving the quick jump of his hips.

"I think I've wanted to do this since I first met you," she said, then she slid her mouth over him, relaxed her throat and took him deep, wrapping her tongue around his thick shaft as she tasted him.

He threaded his fingers in her hair, and she sucked harder, pulling back to sweep her tongue around the head before sliding him deep into her mouth again. She cupped his balls, massaging them lightly as she licked and sucked at his shaft.

"Riley—"

She heard the warning in his voice, and it only excited her more. Her panties were damp with wanting him, but she couldn't end this, not yet, not when he was so close.

She drew him even deeper, increasing the pressure on his scrotum. With her tongue, she felt more blood pulse into his cock. He was close, and she wanted him to finish.

"Riley, babe, I'm going to come." His voice was rough, pained.

She moved her hand to stroke the base of him. His hips bucked, and he let out a low moan before releasing himself in her mouth.

When she pulled away, it was with the taste of him still on her tongue, her jaw aching slightly. Between the two reminders, she wouldn't be surprised if she walked around wet all night.

With heavy lids and quickened breath, he helped her slide back onto his lap. She straddled him, pushing away her own needs. It would have felt great to have him inside her, but she'd needed to give him that.

Charlie cupped her face and brushed a thumb over her lips. "You have one wicked mouth on you."

She couldn't have held back her grin if she wanted to. Chaz had led her to believe she wasn't particularly adept at blowjobs. He'd told her it didn't matter, but just knowing he'd felt that way had always made her feel lacking in the bedroom. If she were honest with herself—and she was finding she hadn't been—she'd have to admit that those insecurities had contributed to her decision to stay in a relationship that hadn't measured up.

Charlie brought her face to his and flicked his tongue across her lips.

Riley drew back, surprised.

"What?"

She brought her fingers to her lips. "I just—you don't have to kiss me if that's gross to you after I—"

He brought her mouth to his again, this time treating her to a full, open-mouth kiss. He swept his tongue inside and she moaned. She turned her head, giving him better access. He tasted like champagne and rebellion.

When he pulled away, his eyes were serious. "Why," he asked, "would I think there is anything gross about the taste of me on your lips?" He smiled. "It's about the sexiest thing in the world."

She chuckled and leaned her head on his shoulder. "Thank you, Charlie."

"Jesus, that's it." His chest shook with a silent chuckle.

She leaned back to see his face. "What?"

"It's official. I'm the luckiest man on the planet. I just got the best blowjob of my life and the drop-dead gorgeous woman who gave it is thanking me." He grinned at her. Not the Charlie "the Devil" Singleton seductive smile everyone knew so well, but a kid-in-the-candy-store, honest-to-God grin.

"I think you might be good for me," she said.

"I know I am," he whispered. He'd dropped his hands to her legs, and his fingers were inching up the sensitive skin of her inner thighs.

Riley glanced out the window. "Where are we going?"

Charlie chuckled. "Don't worry. The driver will keep circling around town until I tap on the window to tell him we're ready."

She wanted to press him for more information about their night, but it was hard when his fingers were between her legs, sweeping the edges of her panties. "You knew I wouldn't go for the 'no sex' thing." She drew in a shaky breath as he found her clit with his thumb.

He stroked her through the thin lace, and pleasure ricocheted through her.

She lifted slightly to give him better access. Only when he was throwing her panties to the floor did she realize he'd been untying the sides with one hand while the other distracted her.

Panties discarded, Charlie slid his hand back up the back of her dress and ran his fingers along the exposed curve of her ass. Still straddling him, she lifted to her knees, desperate to give him better access.

Charlie reached for the controls on the door, then above them, the moon roof opened.

"Go on up," he said, tilting his chin to the exposed night.

Riley gaped at him. His fingers were toying with her most sensitive spots, and he wanted her to do what?

He treated her to another grin, slid both hands to her ass, and lifted her.

"Okay, I'm going," she said, shifting from her knees to feet to stand where she straddled him.

She pulled her body through the moon roof, resting her elbows on the top of the limo. The wind whipped through her hair, and she had to smile. Yes, she understood why he wanted her to do this. How many times had she seen people driving down the Strip, sticking their heads out of limos? She'd always wondered what the appeal was. But now she knew. The cool nighttime desert air swept over her warm cheeks as she watched the lights stream by.

"Come up here. It's beautiful!" she shouted down to him.

His only response was his fingers brushing up the inside of her legs. As she felt his hot tongue press against her sex, a giggle escaped her lips. No, *now* she understood.

Her laughter ended when he slid two fingers inside her. She braced herself on either side of the moon roof and let her eyes float closed.

Vegas whipped around her. She let herself drift into the moment. Charlie stroked her below, moving his fingers in even rhythm with his tongue. The heat below her waist contrasted sharply with the cool air against her face.

She forced her eyes open so she could watch the lights as he touched and kissed her. His hands and mouth picked up their pace, stroking her deeper and faster. She clenched around his fingers. Her hips rocked toward him. His tongue left her, and she wanted to cry out. Pressure mounted inside her from where he worked her with his hand.

As they turned a corner, Charlie pressed his mouth against her clit again. His fingers pressed deep inside her. The fountains in front of the Bellagio came into view. He sucked lightly, and she came apart watching the fountain spray into the night sky.

CHAPTER
SEVENTEEN

Charlie helped Riley lower into the seat beside him. Leaning forward, he pressed his lips against hers. "You are amazing," he whispered. And he meant it.

He was rock hard again after having his mouth on her, tasting her sex, and driving her to orgasm. When it came to Riley, he couldn't get enough. He didn't want to.

He ended the kiss as he tapped on the glass that separated them from the driver.

Riley's eyes went wide, and she scrambled to adjust her dress. Charlie found her panties and handed the scrappy lace to her. Buying Riley lingerie led down only the best roads, and he was already dreaming up what to buy next.

She pulled the panties up over her hips. Her hands flew to her hair, dark and mussed around her face. "I must look like I just walked out of a windstorm."

The limo came to a stop, and Charlie pulled her into a final deep kiss. When he pulled away, she was gasping for breath. "You look beautiful."

Her hand went to her mouth. "Why do I doubt your judgment?"

Charlie gave her a wicked grin. "Because I think you're most beautiful when you look freshly fucked?"

Her eyes went wide.

Just then, the door clicked as someone lifted the handle. Riley scrambled to put herself at rights.

"Trust me," Charlie said, climbing out of the limo. He ducked his head back in and extended his hand for hers. "Every woman in that place is going to wish she looked as beautiful as you."

Riley's shoulders dropped, relaxing, and her eyes softened. "How do you do that?"

She took his hand, and he squeezed her fingers as he led her out. "Do what?" he asked, guiding her arm through his.

"How do you always know just what to say?"

He squeezed her hand where it wrapped around his bicep. "Ever gambled before?" he asked, changing the subject.

She shook her head. "Never in someone else's casino, at least."

Charlie raised a brow then grinned. "Buckle in, sweetheart. You're about to have the night of your life."

As they stepped into the casino, Charlie watched her carefully. Would she be able to take off her managerial hat and see a ritzy casino through the eyes of a patron?

Men and women leaning over tables, throwing dice, dealers turning cards, waitresses squeezing through the crowds with trays full of drinks.

The crowd squeezed at them and Charlie repositioned himself behind her, wrapping his arms around her waist and putting his mouth against her ear. "See that couple playing blackjack? The woman in the blue dress?"

Riley nodded.

"They got kicked out of Grand Escape for counting cards a couple nights ago."

"Why do people come to casinos to get rich? Don't they know they're meant for fun, not income?"

He chuckled and squeezed her tight. "So, what's your game?"

Her teeth sank into her kiss-swollen lower lip before she turned in his arms. She tilted her head up and looked into his eyes. "Would you believe me if I said I've never actually played? Not for real money." Her gaze dropped to his mouth.

Was she thinking of what they'd done in the car? Charlie couldn't get his mind off it, and he'd be walking around uncomfortable all night. Not that he was complaining. "Why not?"

She shrugged. "If you don't play, you get to keep your money. If you play, there's a good chance you'll lose it. It was never much of a question."

"That's why you only play with money you intend to lose."

"Okay." She nodded. "I could probably spend—"

He put a finger to her lips. "Riley, don't spoil my evening and bruise my ego in one swoop. Let me treat you."

She bit her lip again. The gesture made him crazy, made him want to run his tongue along her swollen lip, suck it into his mouth, bite it himself. "Please," he said, his voice coming out rough.

"Okay…" She looked around them. "What's fun?"

He shrugged. "Depends on your personality. We have to find your game."

He took her to the roulette wheel first. He loved watching her big green eyes widen as the wheel spun, loved holding her from behind as she called her bet.

"This isn't my game," she whispered in his ear after a few rounds.

Her lips brushed his ear as she spoke, shooting fire through his veins. He nodded to the wheel. "But you won," he said, wrapping a hand around her hip and pulling her closer.

She grinned and snuggled into him. "It's not about the money."

Next, they tried craps, and when that didn't suit, he took her to a blackjack table.

"We're getting warmer," she said after a few rounds.

Charlie leaned in to tip the dealer and then swept her away from the table.

"Why do you keep looking at your watch?" she asked. "Am I boring you?"

Charlie grinned. "Not a chance, but we have plans. In fact, would you mind if we left the casino for a bit?"

She looked up at him, smiling. "For limo sex?"

He groaned and closed his eyes for a few seconds. "For dancing," he said when he recovered.

He took her hand and she followed him out of the casino and into a grand marble lobby.

"Riley Carter!" The man called her name and began flashing pictures at the same moment. "Rumor has it you're engaged to be married to your long-time boyfriend, Chaz Spencer. What are you doing with Charlie Singleton?"

Charlie instinctively shielded Riley with his body. "Get out of here!"

She squeezed his arm. "It's okay, Charlie."

He turned and the camera kept flashing. "Are you sure?"

She lifted her palms. "We're adults on a date. We're not doing anything wrong."

He looked down at her then—at her big green eyes, her soft smile. Something tightened in his chest. "I'm not sure what your father is going to think about you cavorting with some good-for-nothing poker player," he said. He tried to keep the smile in his voice but failed, too much of his insecurity seeping into his words.

She slipped her hand behind his neck and into his hair. "Do you care what my father thinks?"

"No." The word was exhaled as his attention shifted from her eyes to her lips. "Only you."

With a smile that told him he'd given the right answer, she lifted on her toes and brought her mouth to his.

Charlie met her halfway, knowing they were making the day of the asshole with the camera, and not caring because right now Riley was kissing him. She was kissing him even knowing that, come tomorrow morning, the whole world would be privy to this moment.

He swept his tongue into her mouth and pulled her tight.

Only after he let her go did Riley step back, her lips red, her cheeks flushed.

"Are you two an item?" the pap member asked.

"We're—" Charlie wasn't sure how to answer that question.

"We're having fun," Riley finished for him, and judging by

the proud smile she flashed over her shoulder, she thought he'd approve of her answer. And he did. Riley deserved fun, and that was precisely what he'd set out to give her.

Except, he wanted more.

I love you. She'd typed those words to him last night, and he wanted to hear them again, but this time from her lips.

...

CHAZ STOPPED dancing when he saw Riley enter the club. When Brandy continued grinding against him, he gripped her arm and dragged her to the edge of the dance floor.

"Can't wait for me?" she asked, her words breathy to show him how turned on she was. Which was bullshit, of course. The only thing in Chaz's pants that turned Brandy on were the large bills in his wallet.

Not that this upset him. They'd been fucking for months with the understanding that she would get pretty things and he would get pussy.

He narrowed his eyes and watched over Brandy's shoulder as a woman in red walked up the stairs to the tables that overlooked the dance floor. "Is that—"

Brandy took a step forward and pressed her mouth to his.

He pushed at her shoulders, making her stumble backwards. "Get off my *dick* for a minute, would you?"

Chaz turned to follow Riley's path through the club, ignoring the daggers Brandy was throwing with her eyes.

"I'll be damned," he muttered, heading to the stairs.

"Hey! Where ya going?" Brandy called to his back.

He ignored her. Seeing Riley was enough of a reminder of where sleeping with trash had gotten him.

He made his way to the stairs. Had that really been her? She'd looked...different. Riley had always had a hot bod, but she was skilled at hiding it with the most boring clothes. But tonight... tonight she wore red and a smile and walked like a woman who'd been well fucked.

By the time he reached the top of the stairs, she was at the railing, leaning on her elbows and watching the bodies teeming on the dance floor below.

"I wondered if you'd come find me tonight," he said, wrapping an arm around her.

Her attention jerked to him and she pulled back, eyes widening.

Chaz frowned. "That's why you're here, right?" He'd gone to her apartment at nine, but Lacey had told him Riley was out. That was *all* the bitch would tell him, and she wouldn't even open the door.

"Why would you think that?"

Ignoring the question, he smiled and tucked a lock of hair behind her ear. "You look beautiful tonight." A little too slutty for the future mother of their children, but they could talk about that after they'd ironed everything out between them.

"Chaz." She recoiled from his touch. "I'm here with someone else."

Chaz dropped his hand to his side and clenched it. "Who?" Not that he really had to ask. He knew. She was with the same loser she'd been pictured with in the paper. The same loser she'd been spotted with in the Grand Escape lobby after she'd stopped by Chaz's place. The loser who was responsible for her decision not to wear his ring.

"Does that really matter?" She frowned. "We're over, Chaz. I'm not yours anymore."

He set his jaw. "Because of last night."

She nodded. "In part. But truthfully, I should have ended this a long time ago." She looked over her shoulder, for that poker player no doubt. "Tell me the truth—were you really *happy*?"

"Of course—"

"No, think about it. Were you happy with *me*? And before you answer, ask yourself why you were sleeping with another woman if our relationship was really enough for you."

Chaz cursed himself for getting sloppy. How many months had he insisted Brandy not come to his house? After a while it had just seemed easier to have her over. Since—before last night—Riley wasn't the type to stop by unannounced, he hadn't seen the harm in it. But it had been a fucking careless gamble after years of strategically placing himself in Riley's life.

"I made a mistake, Riley," and damn did he mean it. "Don't let my mistake ruin everything we've worked so hard for." His eyes dropped down the length of her body. "I just can't get over the way you're dressed. Did he ask you to dress like this?"

She released a long breath and took another slight step away from him. "Charlie doesn't tell me how to dress."

Chaz raised a brow. "I hear he buys you lingerie. Sounds to me like he doesn't just tell you, he makes sure it happens."

"That's different." Her brow creased in a deep frown.

"I'll leave you alone to enjoy your evening. But first—as the man who has loved you for two years—I think I deserve to know how things started between you two. I mean, you and I just broke up last night."

"Do we have to talk that kiss to death? I shouldn't have kissed him before you and I were over, but it happened."

He shook his head. "Not the kiss. Before that."

She wrapped her arms around herself and her face grew tight. "What are you trying to suggest? That I was sleeping around?"

"There's more than one way to be unfaithful."

Riley winced then looked at the floor. "Your numbers got mixed up in my new cell phone," she said. "I thought I was texting you, but I was really…" She trailed off.

Chaz felt like he'd been sucker punched. Singleton had gotten her through fucking text messages. "Did he know you thought you were texting me?"

"How would he have known?"

"How do you know he's not the one who switched the numbers?"

She dropped her arms and shook her head. "No. He has no idea. He's not like that, Chaz. Not at all."

Chaz gave her a soft smile and reached for her hand. "I know you like this guy, but he makes a living reading people and taking advantage when opportunity presents itself."

"Chaz—"

He held up his hands. "I won't say more. Just…don't get hurt."

She tugged her hand away. "I won't."

He shook his head. "You just have to forgive me for wanting to protect the heart of the woman I love."

"You don't have to protect my heart, Chaz. Me and Charlie… it's not like that."

Chaz held back his smile. If it wasn't like that, then it wasn't too late for him. Out of the corner of his eye, he saw Charlie approaching, so he took the moment to dip and brush a kiss across Riley's mouth.

She took a step back just as his lips touched hers. "I'm not your girl anymore, Chaz."

"Indulge me in the fantasy that I might be able to win you back." His words were whispered. Emotions skittered across her face. He hadn't lost her yet.

"Riley?"

Guilt masked her features as she swung around to Charlie. *Another point for Team Chaz.*

CHAPTER
EIGHTEEN

Riley looked angelic while she slept. Her dark hair was mussed from their love making, her lips still swollen, but her features were peaceful. As he watched the steady rise and fall of her chest, something unfamiliar tightened his chest.

He should get back to his room and review tapes of competitors. UltimatePokerPowerhouse.net had made an offer, but it had been a low one, unsubstantial, barely enough to cover the entry fee. If Rick couldn't work his magic and get Charlie a better deal, Charlie's career would depend on a tournament win. Without it, he wouldn't be able to afford to continue.

Even knowing what lay on the line, he couldn't tear himself away from her. When he'd seen Chaz kissing her tonight, he'd felt something.

Primitive, territorial jealousy over seeing another man kiss the woman he was sleeping with—yes, but that was to be expected. And he'd felt that in spades. But he'd also felt something more. He didn't want any other man touching her, true, but the bigger threat had been the way they'd looked at each other, the fear that she might feel something for this man that Charlie wanted her to feel for him.

He'd taken Riley to Tango to enjoy the thing she loved most, and he'd been too damn stubborn to let Chaz change his plans. Moving together on the dance floor had been as natural as flowing water. Riley's body had rubbed against his as they danced, and her mouth kept him wanting as it hovered millimeters from the sensitive skin on his neck. Her hands had hooked into his belt, held him close—as if he wanted to be anywhere else.

Now she slept, sated after a night of fun, sex, and indulgence. He liked having her like this—sleeping, peaceful, tangled in sheets in her bed, not in some big hotel's high-roller suite or in a bed big enough to lose her in the middle of the night. He was sick of hotels. He wanted a home—not the sterile condo he owned in LA. He wanted a house in Vegas, with a yard and a dog. He wanted a chance to get to know that cocky teen who was as sneaky as he was lanky and who knew far too much about women for his age. He wanted Riley.

I love you.

He hadn't missed that she hadn't said it again since the text. Was she afraid she'd scare him off? Hell, he hadn't even replied. She had no way of knowing he gave a shit.

He brushed her hair back with his fingertips. His poker career was disintegrating before his eyes, and when it was over, Charlie Singleton would claim his birthright as just another nobody.

How could he tell Riley Carter he'd fallen in love with her when shame was just around the bend?

...

"You gonna start helping with the rent?"

Charlie filled a glass of water and grinned at Lacey. His sister sat at the kitchen table in her pajamas, looking none too happy about being awake. "Morning, Lace," Charlie said with a smile. Normally he didn't believe in smiling before eight a.m., but he'd slept with Riley in his arms last night, and it had felt damn good.

"You could at least get that shit-eating grin off your face," she said, yawning. "It's too early for new love's bliss."

Charlie cast a glance at Riley's bedroom door to make sure he and his sister were alone. "What makes you think I'm in love?"

She leaned back and crossed her arms. "Well, aren't you?"

Charlie swallowed. "It's complicated."

Lacey unfolded the newspaper sitting in front of her with a knowing "Humph."

"What's that supposed to mean?" he asked.

"Nothing." She snapped open the paper and thumbed through it. "You don't need to tell me anything. I'm just your *only sister* and—" Her eyes went wide. "Oh, crap."

"What?"

She turned the paper so he could see the picture that graced the front of the Society section.

"Oh. That."

"Do you think Riley will be upset?"

Charlie shrugged. "She practically posed for the guy."

"And the caption doesn't bother you?"

Charlie snagged the paper from Lacey's hands and read the caption. *Has Vegas' Good Daughter fallen from grace to consort with "the Devil"?*

He sighed. "I'm used to this crap, but Riley's not."

"Riley's not what?" the beauty in question asked, sidling into the kitchen and making a beeline for the coffee.

Charlie hadn't even heard her emerge from the bedroom. "You're not used to the bullshit press." He handed her the paper. "I'm sorry about this."

She scanned it quickly, then dropped it on the table. "If that's their best shot at us, I think we'll be okay."

Us. Charlie took her arm and pulled her to him, drawing her into his embrace before lowering his mouth to hers.

"Yuck!" Lacey said. "Hello, I'm thrilled for you two and everything, but it's way too early to watch my brother suck face with my best friend."

Charlie ignored her and kissed the woman he loved.

...

CHARLIE WAS waiting at Angela's office door when she arrived at work.

Her dark eyes widened and her hand flew to her chest. "How'd you get back here?"

Charlie smirked. "You have a *very* sweet girl working the front counter."

"Jesus." Angela shook her head and unlocked her office. Entering, she hung her purse on the back of the door and straightened her suit before looking back to him. "I thought we agreed we'd let the lawyers handle this."

Charlie raised his brows. "*We* didn't agree on anything."

Angela bit her lip, turning away from him again and heading toward her desk. She fumbled with papers there as she spoke. "Listen, I don't want this to be a big deal. I really hate drama."

"You sprang a grown child on me out of the blue. Did you expect me to smile, write you a check, and walk away?"

She shook her head. "I didn't have a choice. Tony, he has college coming up and—"

"Does he go by that name? Tony?"

"What?"

Charlie shrugged. "It's just that he told me his name was Derrick."

She pulled back defensively and her face drew taut. "When did you meet Tony? Why did you arrange that without my knowledge?" She scrambled for her purse, pulling out her phone. "I swear, Singleton, you can't pull this shit. My lawyer—"

"*He* found *me*, Angela." He grabbed a frame from her desk and turned it so he could see the picture. Sure enough, "Derrick" smiled back at him. "He's a good kid," Charlie said softly, lowering the frame back to the desk.

"Charlie, you think long and hard before you make my son believe you're going to be this great father figure he's never had. You can't just—" She collapsed into her chair and pulled a hand through her hair. "Think about someone other than yourself for a minute."

Charlie clenched his fists. "Jesus, Angela." He fought the sudden urge to hit something. "What the hell do you want? He's my *son*. The boy deserves a father."

She raised her gaze to meet his, and her eyes were pleading. "And what about when you take off for months at a time, Charlie? Who's going to be his father then?"

"You can't keep him from me. Hell, *you* had the court come after me, and now *he's* reaching out to me. Did it occur to you that *you* are the one making this more difficult than it needs to be?"

She didn't respond, and Charlie let the silence stretch between them.

Angela spoke first. "Do you remember what you once told me about your father?" When he didn't answer, she looked up at him, wetting her lips. "You said staying out of your life was the best thing he ever did for you. Tony's a good kid. He has a bright future. Think about it."

CHAPTER
NINETEEN

*L*acey's *out for the evening, so we have the place to ourselves.*

Charlie dropped into a chair in the lobby of Grand Escape to answer Riley's text. He couldn't help the smile that tugged at his lips as his thumbs pecked out the message. *What do you have in mind?*

Her message came quickly. *Any number of things that involve your hands and mouth would be just fine by me.*

He grinned. He liked her way of thinking, but he wanted to woo her as much as he wanted to ravish her. *Let me take you out to a late dinner and we'll go from there.*

Dessert first, dinner later.

Shit. To hell with good intentions. *Put on something from your collection to inspire me.*

You're really coming over?

What man could say no to that invitation?

"Hey, Singleton!"

Charlie looked up to see Griminski, the surveillance officer, crossing the lobby, an envelope in his hand. Charlie stood and extended a hand. "How are things?"

"Same shit, different day. You know the story," Griminski said with a smile. He looked over each shoulder and lowered his voice. "Boss told me to destroy this, but I thought you might want it." He squeezed Charlie's forearm with nearly bruising force. "Tell anyone and I'll get my ass canned, but I still felt like we owed you. Anyway, I can tell she's important to you."

Charlie looked down at the envelope Griminski offered. He could think of only one thing that could be inside. "Are you serious?"

The guy lifted his hands in innocence. "Anyone asks and I destroyed it. Understand?"

He nodded, thoughts of Riley, a negligee, and their personal sex tape tangling in his head. "I understand completely." He took the envelope. "Thanks, Martin. You're not bad."

...

CHARLIE ARRIVED at Riley's door and waited as patiently as he could for her answer.

"I'm coming!" she called seconds before she cracked the door open.

"I was hoping you'd wait for me before doing that," Charlie said.

Her eyes widened in approval at the sight of him.

He trailed his gaze over her body. She was wearing an old, yellow terry cloth robe. It was tattered, had a hole in the elbow and a torn seam. So how was it he'd never seen anyone look so sexy? Was it the flushed cheeks and bright green eyes...or the promise of what might be underneath that robe?

She slid her hands under the buttons of his shirt, then pulled him into her apartment. The second the door shut, she was on him, hands at his belt, her mouth at his neck.

He groaned. "That's one hell of a greeting, but if you have what I think you do under that robe, I'll be damned if I'm going to let you rush me."

She laughed but persisted at his belt.

Charlie stopped her hands, giving her fingertips a gentle squeeze. "Before you get too carried away, I think I have something you might want to see."

With a grin, she unzipped his pants and slid her hand inside. She pressed the palm of her hand against his erection. "You have something I want to see, all right."

Before she could distract him further, he slid the DVD case in front of her face.

She raised a brow and stilled her hand. "Mood music?"

"Apparently, your father told the surveillance manager to destroy this. Griminski thought I might like to keep it."

Her jaw dropped as she looked at the case, then back up at him. "So that's...?"

"It is."

She tugged her bottom lip between her teeth. "What are you going to do with it?"

He backed away from her, aware she was watching his every move as he put the DVD in the player.

"Charlie, I don't think I want to see—"

"Don't you?"

Her cheeks flushed a deep red. "I haven't done anything like this before."

Charlie grabbed the remote and pressed play. The screen showed Riley wrapped in his arms, him whispering in her ear and kissing the column of her neck.

Charlie dropped the remote on the couch and positioned himself behind her.

"This is embarrassing," she said softly.

He snaked his arm around her to the tie on her robe, parting it with flick of his wrist and exposing beautiful breasts, brimming at the top of thin black lace.

His gaze flickered between Riley on the screen—clawing at his shirt, frantic—and the Riley in his arms—breath accelerating, her hard nipples pressing against lace.

He pressed his mouth to her neck. She swallowed hard as his hand cupped her breast, his fingers toying with her puckered nipple.

He pressed his other hand flat against her belly, pulling her closer to him, letting her feel his erection at her back.

She gasped. Charlie didn't know if the gasp came from the work of his fingers of the sight of him on screen, sinking to his haunches and pressing his face between her legs.

He slipped his hand lower, cupping her swollen sex. He moved his mouth to her ear. "I can feel how wet you are through your panties."

Her breath hitched, and he maneuvered under the lace, wanting to feel her slick, wet flesh against his fingers.

Her lids fluttered closed as he slid a finger into her, but she opened them again, watching the screen, mesmerized by the erotic images there. She was so wet on his fingers, so tight as she pulsed around him. He wanted to be inside her.

Charlie withdrew his hand, and she whimpered in protest. He pulled her robe over her shoulders and let it drop to the floor. He drew in a sharp breath at the sight of her.

In thigh-highs and black lace panties that exposed more ass than they covered, she was a wet dream. The heat in her eyes as she looked over her shoulder filled him with unexpected tenderness.

She turned to him and slowly unbuttoned his shirt. When it hung open, she ran her fingers along the path of fine hair that tapered down from his chest and over his abdomen.

"You do something to me," he said, his voice coming out rough. "No one. Never before." Emotion sat like thick cotton in his throat, keeping the words from forming right.

She grinned. "And here I thought you were a seasoned lover."

"I'm not talking about sex," he said.

She pressed her lips to the tender spot on the side of his neck and molded herself to him until his erection pressed into her belly. "Well, why not?"

He dropped his head to kiss her, to tell her with lips and tongue just what she meant to him. He trailed his lips along her jaw line and down to her throat. The sound of her moan had him closing his eyes and praying for patience he didn't feel.

"Your mouth might not be talking about sex, but other parts of you sure are."

He silenced her with another kiss, sweeping his tongue into her mouth and tasting his fill of her. By the time he pulled away, she was breathless and tugging off his shirt. Gone was the teasing siren. Riley wanted him, and she wanted him now. He planned to use that to his fullest advantage.

He led her to the floor. She kept her green eyes locked on him as he carefully settled beside her.

Shackling her wrists in one hand, he traced lines down the center of her body with the other. She released another sweet moan, arching her hips.

He slipped his hand between her legs, circling her sex where he knew she wanted him to touch. She squirmed in protest. "Has any other man ever made you feel this way, Riley?"

"No, never." She swiveled her hips in a vain attempt to guide his hand where she wanted it.

"You want me, don't you?"

She licked her lips. "Yes."

He leaned in close and flicked his tongue against her ear. "I want you."

She swallowed hard. "Then what are you waiting for?"

It was a good question. The words were on the tip of his tongue: *I love you, Riley*, but they refused to budge from their spot.

How many men made it to thirty-two without falling in love? Charlie had, and now he hadn't just fallen, he'd plunged face first.

"I can't believe how much I want to be inside you again," he murmured in her ear.

"Then do it," she begged.

He shed his pants quickly and settled over her, weight on his elbows. Then he shifted, remembering an important detail. "I forgot to bring condoms," he said. "Do you have any?"

"I'm on the pill," she whispered. "And I'm okay. Healthy. Are you…?"

Charlie swallowed hard, nodding. "You're sure?" The idea of being inside Riley like that appealed too damn much. Their gazes tangled as he slid into her—skin to skin for the first time.

She was so hot and wet and tight, and it felt so incredible to be in her, to be moving without any barrier between them. He slowed, trying to last longer than his building pleasure would allow.

"No," she whispered, her nails digging into his shoulder blades. "Faster."

He pushed himself up so he could look into her eyes as he rocked into her, so he could watch the pleasure on her face.

She wrapped her legs around his waist and threw her head back, her eyes fluttering closed.

Her nails dug into her shoulder blades as the orgasm took her and she convulsed around him. His own pleasure climbed, and his cock swelled more than he thought possible, spurred by direct contact with her hot, wet sex.

When he came inside her, it was she who cried out.

He allowed himself several long moments to recover. Burying his head in the crook of her neck, he breathed in the sweet, clean scent of her. She smelled like a cool spring day with clear skies and laundry on the line. She smelled like home.

He carefully slid out of her and rolled to his side. "I've never done that before," he said softly. He brought her hand to his lips and kissed the back of it. "Thank you."

She turned and smiled at him, her green eyes soft. "Which part? The quickie part or the no condom part?"

He chuckled. "My male pride insists I lie to you and tell you I've never blown my load so quickly, but I believe we have video evidence proving otherwise."

She laughed, her fingers running lazy trails over his chest. "And you even wore a condom...then?"

A lock of her hair had fallen in her face, and Charlie brushed it behind her ear, reading her question in her eyes. "I wore a condom every time. Even with Angela."

"Angela is...?"

"My son's mother." The word *son* still felt strange attached to him, more like playing pretend than talking about his real life.

She let out a long breath. "So he *is* yours."

Charlie nodded. "He looks just like me and the numbers make sense."

"How old is he?"

"Sixteen. About the age I was when he was conceived." Charlie smiled, thinking of Tony. "He's a good kid. A little sneaky, but only because he knows what he wants."

She smiled, her green eyes soft. "What's it like, having a child? You know, flesh of your flesh and all that?"

Charlie propped himself up on an elbow. He wanted a better view of her as they talked about this part of his life, as he shared this vulnerable piece of himself. "I don't really know. I wasn't given the opportunity to be his father. Angela must have been pregnant when I left town, but I didn't know, and she never contacted me again until I was served with those papers."

Riley sat up, her cheeks flushing. "How could she do that? You had a right to know."

Charlie sighed. He pushed himself off the floor and offered her a hand. When they stood face to face, he pressed his lips to hers. Her indignation on his behalf warmed long-ago-hardened places inside him.

"What was that for?" she asked when he pulled away.

He grinned. "Just for believing in me." Then with a sigh, he explained, "Angela thought it was best for Tony if I wasn't part of his life. Given the circumstances—that I was a high school dropout bent on living life on my own terms and no one else's—maybe she was right."

Riley shook her head. "I don't believe it. Not for a minute. You're a good man, and, ready or not, you were the child's father. She stole sixteen years from you."

"Is that what you think about those years your father wasn't in your life?"

Riley flinched, then slipped away from him and walked around to sit on the couch. Charlie followed her, sitting beside her but saying nothing. "It's not his fault. Not completely. My mom told him she didn't need his money or his help."

"How did you feel about that?" Charlie asked softly.

"I didn't know any better until after she died. I guess then it occurred to me that he should have pushed the issue. He was my father, why didn't he insist on visitation?"

Charlie reached for her hand and squeezed it in his.

"And it might have occurred to me that the transition after her death would have been easier if he hadn't been a stranger to me. My whole like would have been different if I'd known him, been sure of his love before he was the only one I had."

"Do you think you'd be dancing for a living now…if you hadn't been bent on proving yourself to your father?"

She blinked at him. "It's not easy to make a living as a dancer."

He turned on the couch and drew her to him so she was leaning against his chest. "That's not what I asked."

"I think we all have a dream of…what we could have been," she said softly. "Except maybe you—fancy professional poker player." She tilted her chin up and grinned at him.

"Maybe we're both too scared to go after what we really want."

She turned in his arms and put her hand against his face, studying him. "What do you want, Charlie?"

"I want…" *You.* "…a way out of the poker life. Another career opportunity that would let me stay here, near Tony."

"Like what?"

"I don't know yet. I'm a little worried there's nothing else I'm any good at." It was embarrassing to say it out loud, but he knew he could tell Riley the truth. Lacing his fingers through hers, Charlie watched her carefully. "Would you like to meet my son?"

She didn't recoil or pull away. Instead her eyes lit with excitement, her pink lips curved up at the corners. "Really? You want me to meet him?"

"Yeah. I do. I don't want to fuck this up." He gave her a sheepish grin and pressed his lips to the back of her hand. "Maybe you could come and slap me upside the head every time I act as a bad role model."

She laughed. "Sure. What's the plan?"

"He's going to meet us at Grand Escape for a game of poker."

CHAPTER
TWENTY

"So, is that kid going to join us tonight or not?" Ashton, one of Charlie's poker buddies, asked the next night. Ashton deftly shuffled cards, not bothering to watch his hands. Showing off, as always.

Charlie, Riley, and Ashton sat in a private reserved poker room at Grand Escape waiting for Derrick or Tony or whatever the hell the kid wanted to call himself.

But Charlie's son hadn't showed.

Charlie looked at his watch. "Go ahead and start. We can always deal him in later."

Riley cocked her head, grinning. "Maybe his mom didn't like the idea of you teaching her son how to gamble?"

Charlie squeezed her hand—hell, was he actually nervous about this?—and shrugged. "It's not like we're playing for real money. Pretending gambling doesn't exist doesn't keep kids from doing it. I'd rather he understand the risks."

Under the table, she squeezed his thigh. "I think it was sweet of you to set this up."

Not that it would matter if Tony didn't show. Charlie ignored the disappointment niggling at his gut. Maybe Tony was running late. Or maybe something had come up.

"You lovebirds ready to play?" Across the table, Ashton shuffled the cards and gave Riley a once-over. "Tell me you're not really dating this loser," he said, nodding to Charlie.

Riley reached back for Charlie's hand. "I suppose you think I should be with someone else?"

"Sure," Ashton said, "someone who knows a good hand from his own ass would be a good starting point."

Charlie snorted. "Easy to talk shit when nothing's on the line. Ry, if this were a real game, we'd walk out of here with all that cocky son-a-bitch's money."

"He's just jealous because he hasn't won a championship in months," Ashton said, "and nobody wants to pony up to sponsor him anymore."

Riley frowned and cast a glance at Charlie. "Why do you need sponsors?"

"They pay the high fees for the tournaments and pay us for wearing their name like a human billboard," Ashton explained.

"It's not so bad," Charlie said. "It's a good way to make a living doing this." And it was the only way he knew how to make a living at all.

"Especially if you aren't good enough to win," Ashton said.

"If you didn't blow your money on women and gambling, you wouldn't *have* to win them all to make a living," Charlie said.

Ashton dealt the cards and smiled at Riley. "So are you going to be Singleton's next Nicole Abucee?"

Riley narrowed her gaze. Charlie tensed and flashed Ashton a warning glare.

Ashton ignored him. "His agent seems to think he needs another scandal to raise his appeal to the sponsors. Those pictures of you two in the paper were the best career bump this washed-up talent has had in a year."

Riley cut her gaze to Charlie again.

"My agent's an idiot," Charlie said. "Apparently the only thing they taught him in that fancy MBA program of his is 'sex sells.'"

"He's right," Ashton said after they paid their blinds. "So, are you the Devil's new scandal?"

"Why?" Riley asked, looking Ashton in the eye. "Are you jealous?"

Ashton chuckled. "Nah, it's just that UltimatePokerPowerhouse. net finally got sick of dicking around with Singleton's agent and gave the sponsorship to that new little shit—Little Jimmi?"

The air left Charlie's lungs in a *whoosh*. He dropped his cards. "They did what?" Fuck. Why hadn't Rick called?

The smile dropped from Ashton's face. "Shit, man, they didn't tell you? That's low." He gave a forced smile. "It's okay. I'm sure our man here has some sort of backup sponsor."

Charlie swallowed hard. He didn't. Of course he didn't. Who wanted him?

"It doesn't pay to play without a sponsor," Ashton explained.

"Unless you win, right?" Riley said.

Ashton shrugged. "It's not about skill anymore, not with the fucking internet amateurs changing the game so much. They play like they're betting dimes, not thousands." He shook his head. "All the strategy is gone."

Charlie pushed back from the table. He needed some fresh air. The room was too damn hot. Too damn small.

"Charlie?" Riley put her hand on his arm. "You okay?"

Charlie forced himself to wink at her and smile. "Sounds like I need to call my agent. You'll excuse me?"

She narrowed her gaze. "Sure."

Charlie couldn't get out of the room fast enough. By the time he'd reached the street, he'd fished his cell out of his pocket and pressed the memory for Rick. He hung up when he got the man's voicemail.

Charlie paced down a block and back, his blood pressure rising. It wasn't about the money. He wouldn't be out on the street tomorrow if he never had another sponsor. He could sell his condo in LA and pull from his savings, but it wasn't enough to retire on. He was thirty-two. If poker was done with him, what the hell was he supposed to do with the rest of his life?

His phone rang and he quickly took the call. "Rick, what the hell is going on?"

"Singleton, I've been trying to get a hold of you, buddy."

"Could have fooled me."

"Don't be like that, Charlie. I called your suite and left you messages."

Charlie hadn't been there. He'd been with Riley. Nevertheless, it was a piss-poor excuse when Rick knew his cell number. "So you lost the deal?" He resumed his pacing, anxious for his agent to get to the part where he explained that everything would be okay.

"Man, I hate that it had to go down like this, but we're just not working out."

Charlie froze in middle of the sidewalk. Someone slammed into his back and muttered a few choice words. "You're *firing* me?"

"Maybe another agent could do better for you. I'm sorry it had to come out like this. Like I said, I called your room last night after I put the letter in the mail."

In other words, he'd done everything he could to avoid talking to Charlie while still being able to swear he "tried." "Just one question, Rick."

"What's that?" Rick sounded bored with the conversation already.

"Little Jimmi wouldn't happen to be a new client of yours, would he?"

"Charlie, that has nothing to do with this."

"I've heard enough." Charlie ended the call before slinking down to the nearest available bench. People buzzed by him, strolling down the sidewalk to see the next Vegas sight. Maybe that couple was going to Cirque du Soleil, another heading to the blackjack tables. Every one of them walked with purpose. They knew who they were and where they were going.

He didn't realize Riley had come out to find him until her fingers brushed his arm. "Is everything okay?"

Charlie blew out a breath, running a hand through his hair. "Did Tony show?"

Riley frowned and shook her head, her green eyes filling with pity. "I'm sorry."

Maybe it was better this way. Better to end his relationship with his son before it started, better not to form a bond and have one more person watch as Charlie spiraled into a nobody.

"Ashton said you'd find another sponsor," Riley said, squeezing his arm. "It's going to be okay."

Ashton didn't know what the hell he was talking about. Charlie had done his best not to let anyone know just what a *persona non grata* he'd been to the sponsors. "I'm sorry about those pictures," he said, placing his hand on top of hers. He swallowed hard, a fist of emotion blocking his throat. "I thought a couple pictures of us together would save my career. Looks like I was wrong."

She pulled her hand away and straightened. "What?"

Charlie lifted his gaze. Riley's face was etched with hurt. She sat stone still. "You told them to take pictures?"

Something rabid gnawed at his gut, and again he tried to swallow around that fist. "I thought it could help us both. Chaz was bad for you and I needed some press." He reached for her hand. "It was stupid and it didn't help anything."

Riley yanked her hand away. "You're right. It was stupid."

"Riley—"

She shook her head and took a step back. "No. Don't." Then she turned on her heel and walked away.

...

RILEY STORMED up the stairs to her apartment. She'd taken a cab home, anxious to get away from Charlie. Their first kiss, the one that had changed her whole life, had been nothing but a publicity stunt. Something good for the cameras. The knowledge ground at her heart, rubbed across it with the finesse of a cheese grater.

She turned her key in the lock and pushed through the door. She froze at the male silhouette on her couch. Forcing herself to move, she hit the lights fast. "Chaz, you scared the crap out of me."

Chaz stood, smoothing his pants. "I didn't mean to, but we need to talk."

She placed a hand to her pounding heart. "You can't just come into my apartment uninvited anymore." She crossed to him and extended a hand, palm up. "Give me the key back."

Chaz frowned. "You're still upset about what you walked in on the other night, aren't you?"

Riley dropped her hand and took a step back. She didn't want to be this close to him. She was sick of Chaz, and now Charlie had betrayed her too. Catholic nuns were on to something, and it wasn't fashion. "You're nothing to me anymore, Chaz," she said, softly so he might understand she spoke truth, not melodrama.

Chaz gave her a tentative smile. "I know I screwed up royally, but don't throw this away. You're too mature to—"

"Don't tell me what I am." She wrapped her arms around herself. She was done being screwed over by the men she loved. She looked into Chaz's eyes—eyes she used to think were so warm. She couldn't see that warmth anymore. She'd been wrong about him. Had she been wrong about Charlie too? "Our relationship is over. I want that to be clear. Don't hold out for me."

"Just give it some time, Riley. I love you and I'll wait for you. I know I made a mistake, and if that means I have to wait another two years before you are ready to forgive me so we can move on to the next stage of our life—"

Riley clenched her fists and fought the urge to cover her ears. "Enough. Why are you pretending you want me when you only want my money?"

His jaw hardened. "Have you been talking to Charlie?" he asked. "Is he putting ideas in your head?"

She shook her head. "No. I'm just finally wising up."

He tried to smile but it didn't reach the hard edge to his stare.

"I'm not your puppet anymore. I will not be used for you to grow your savings account."

"You're being stupid."

"Get out, Chaz."

"What?"

She wrapped her arms around her waist. "Please. Leave."

"Don't do anything you'll regret, Riley. We could be good together. Think about your father's company! He offered it to me, Riley. If I marry you. We could run it together—"

"Never," she said, knowing now what she'd suspected for two years and never let herself believe. Chaz had never been in love with her. He'd been in love with her father's money.

Chaz pushed to his feet, disgust evident on his face. "This is the biggest mistake you've ever made."

Riley nodded to a box she'd placed by the door. "I put your stuff in there." She waved toward the DVD tower by the television. "I think some of your movies are in there too. Take what's yours and let yourself out."

She turned on her heel and retreated to her bedroom, closing the door behind her.

TWENTY

CHAPTER

ONE

"What the hell do you want?" Charlie scowled at his ex-agent. The man had balls of steel, showing his face to Charlie before seven a.m., let alone so soon after screwing him over. The man's persistent phone calls to let him up to the limited-access suite had dragged Charlie out of bed. Charlie was un-caffeinated, unrested, and last he checked there was a gaping hole in his chest where his fucking heart used to be.

Under the circumstances, the guy was lucky he still had all his teeth.

Rick pushed through the door and into Charlie's suite, a big-ass smile on his face. "Have you seen the news yet?" He rubbed his hands together. "This was brilliant, man. If I'd known you had this up your sleeve, I wouldn't have broken off our relationship."

Charlie groaned, following him to the TV. Rick grabbed the remote, and Charlie said, "What the hell are you talking about?"

Rick let out a long, hard stream of air and clicked on the television, flipping to a local news station.

"And Nevada unemployment rates dropped by a tenth of a percent this quarter," the newscaster said with a nauseating amount of perk.

Charlie looked to Rick, who said, "Just…wait."

Charlie pulled a hand over his eyes. Hell, he was damned if he was going to wait without coffee. He padded over to the suite's kitchenette and put the pot under the tap. He could kick Rick's traitorous ass post-caffeine.

The male newscaster said, "What does a hotel heir apparent known as Vegas' Good Daughter have in common with a professional poker player known as the Devil? Apparently, a wild streak and access to this penthouse-level elevator."

Charlie dropped the coffee pot. As he swung around, he heard it shatter in the sink. "What the fuck?"

"It's beautiful," Rick said.

The male newscaster continued, "The Grand Escape Resort and Casino's Annual National Poker Tournament begins tomorrow, bringing with it the best professional players in the country, among them Charlie 'the Devil' Singleton."

His female counterpart nodded. "Apparently 'the Devil' can tempt even the best-behaved girls, or so it appears from security tapes anonymously released this morning that feature the couple in a compromising position in the resort's *public* elevator."

"Jesus," Charlie muttered.

"The tapes are too graphic for our wide audience at WRBC, but you can—"

Before she could finish, Charlie snatched the remote from Rick's hands and clicked through the channels. He knew what station wasn't above sharing the alleged tapes. Sure enough, when the dial landed on G! TV, he saw a still shot in the corner of the screen. The network must have taken this shot from the end of their time in the elevator. The picture showed Riley pressed against the elevator wall, her legs wrapped around his waist right above where they'd blurred out his bare ass.

"Riley Carter, daughter of the shrewd Vegas businessman and hotelier Quinton Carter, has been in a serious relationship with Daddy's right-hand man for a couple years now, and was reported to be engaged to her longtime beau, begging the question: Does her man know Vegas' Good Daughter has been consorting with 'the Devil'?"

Charlie clenched a hand. "Jesus, would they get off that already?"

Rick blew out a breath, a smile tugging at the corner of his mouth. "It makes for good news."

"Our investigators are getting reports this morning confirming that the poker player is in the middle of a paternity suit with his high school sweetheart."

"Who isn't this guy sleeping with?" her co-host asked.

"Since Papa Bear Carter is sure to disapprove of her relationship with someone of Singleton's reputation, that seems to be the multimillion-dollar question."

Charlie's stomach clenched. They were making this about Riley. Jesus, he'd been an idiot to be with her in such a public place. "How the hell did they get that tape?"

Rick grinned. "So that's how you're going to play this, huh? Act like you knew nothing about it?"

Charlie scowled. He needed to know so he could find the asshole responsible and castrate him. "How much is out there?"

"The whole elevator ride through the moment you step out the doors. Charlie, it's on TV, in the papers, and, for folks who prefer the uncensored version, all over the internet."

"Fuck."

Rick twirled a cigarette between his fingers. "The tape of you and Hollywood It Girl five years ago gave your career a kick in the ass. But that was nothing compared to this. This is huge. This is—"

Rick stopped speaking as Charlie slammed him against the wall.

...

RILEY DIDN'T believe in conversation before coffee, let alone G! TV. The downside of having a roommate was that sometimes these decisions were out of her hands. Lacey's guilty pleasure was celebrity gossip, and sometimes that meant waking up to news of a Paris Hilton scandal or the latest measurement of J Lo's hips.

Riley groaned but slouched toward the kitchen to pour herself a cup of get-up-and-go. "I don't care who Jennifer Aniston is in love with today. It's way too early for television." Coffee would be her life force this morning. As she'd lain in bed, she'd contemplated rolling over and going back to sleep. She would have called in to work, but her aching heart had refused to let her mind rest, so it would have been a waste of a personal day.

Riley took another gulp of coffee and narrowed her eyes at Lacey, who was glued to the TV and still hadn't responded. "Lace? Are you awake?"

When Lacey looked over her shoulder, she was worrying her bottom lip between her teeth, her brow wrinkled. What did Charlie call that? A tell?

"Riley, I'm so sorry."

Riley frowned. Did Lacey know about her fight with Charlie? "About what?"

"You and Charlie," Lacey said. "It's plastered all over the news."

"Those pictures are old news. So I went on a couple dates with Charlie Singleton. Who cares?" Riley waved a hand dismissively even as a dull ache gnawed at her chest. He'd set up those pictures. He'd used her.

Lacey pushed herself off the couch and gaped at Riley. "You *knew*?"

"Well, sure, I—" A flash of something on the television grabbed Riley's attention. What was she watching?

"Oh my God." Riley's chest collapsed, too small for her pounding heart. Her throat constricted, too small to take in the air she needed.

In a blink, Lacey was off the couch and at Riley's side, taking the coffee from her hand and lowering her into a kitchen chair.

"What—? Is that—?" She couldn't breathe.

"Shh." Lacey pressed a hand against her back. "Put your head between your legs."

Riley did as instructed, her mind spinning. It just didn't make sense.

How did the paparazzi get that tape of her and Charlie in the elevator if Charlie was the only one who had a copy?

...

WHEN CHARLIE arrived at Riley's apartment, Lacey met him at the door, her face a study of worry. Over her shoulder, he could see Riley curled up on the couch, knees drawn up to her chest, eyes glued to the television.

"Has she been like this all morning?" Charlie asked.

Lacey frowned. "Pretty much. I keep trying to turn off the TV, but she just turns it back on." She sighed and eyed her friend. "I'm late for work, but I didn't want to leave her alone."

Charlie squeezed her arm. "Get out of here. I'll take care of her."

Lacey grabbed her purse. "Thanks. See if you can get her to talk. I'm worried."

Charlie nodded, but he waited until his sister pulled the door shut before her before he went to Riley. Settling on the couch beside her, he grabbed the remote and clicked off the TV. "Riley, I'm so sorry." He took her hand in his and waited for her to turn into him, to wrap her arms around his neck. Something to indicate his presence was a comfort to her.

Instead, she stiffened. "Why did you let it leak?"

Her voice was thick with tears, and he wasn't sure he heard her right. "What?"

"The footage." She put her palm to his shoulder, pushing him away. "You said yourself you were the only one who had a copy."

Charlie drew back. "You think *I* did this?"

The way she wrapped her arms around herself was answer enough.

He pushed to his feet and ran a hand through his hair. "You think today's been a joyride for me?" He pointed to the TV. "You think I *enjoyed* this?"

"I bet your phone is ringing off the hook now." She chewed on her bottom lip, tears streaming down her pale face. "Sponsors are probably lining up outside your door with this kind of scandal." She shook her head. "I don't understand how you could do it."

He stared at her for a long minute: her bloodshot eyes, her

dark hair, loose in ringlets around her face, her knees drawn to her chest like she was protecting herself from something. From him. The accusation that he had released the tape was bad enough from Rick, but from Riley it was the knockout blow to his already reeling heart.

"I'm *in love* with you," he said it softly. "I want a life with you. Why would I ruin that?"

The front door flew open and Chaz barreled in. "Riley, I just saw. I can't believe it."

"What's he doing here?" Charlie growled.

Chaz cocked his head, giving Charlie a once-over. "I could say the same about you." He shifted his attention back to Riley. "You told me you were scratching an itch with your bad-boy poker player, but I thought today's developments might prove what a bad idea that was."

Charlie set his jaw. His fists itched to plow into the cocky son-of-a-bitch's face. He looked at Riley. "You want me to get this asshole out of here?"

Riley crossed her arms over her chest. "Chaz, what do you want?"

Chaz's dark eyes hardened. He might be a prick, but he wasn't slow, and he knew he'd taken the wrong tack. "Riley, you can't blame me for being worried. The woman I love is being exploited all over television."

Charlie's hands clenched, but he refused to give Chaz the satisfaction of his response.

"Chaz, enough," Riley said. "This is between me and Charlie."

"You heard her," Charlie said, taking a step toward Chaz. "Leave."

Chaz narrowed in on Charlie. "Lucky for you the numbers on her phone got mixed up. If she'd known it was you on the other end of the—what do the kids call it? Sexting?—you may have never gotten yourself into her pants."

Charlie took another step forward. "What the hell are you talking about?"

Riley hopped off the couch and grabbed the back of Charlie's shirt. "Don't."

Chaz's eyes lit up. "Oh! You didn't know?" He chuckled. "When Riley was texting you, she thought she was texting me. It turns out our numbers were switched on her new phone."

Charlie turned to Riley, waiting for her to deny it. She stood stock still, saying nothing. Charlie wished she'd call Chaz a liar and tell the fucker to leave, but her silence was evidence enough things weren't going to go his way today.

"It's true?" His stomach dropped.

Riley winced. "I should have told you."

He didn't wait for goodbyes, but pushed his way out the door. Flames of bitterness, anger, and resentment burned his stomach and licked their way up his chest.

He was down the second flight of stairs when she called his name. His heart lodged in his throat as he turned around. "Unless you told *Chaz* to go to hell, you don't need to waste your time."

Stopped on the stair above him, she blinked. He could lift his hand and touch her again, feel her soft skin under his fingers just one more time, and it was so damn tempting. But he didn't.

"You should have told me," he said. What an ass he'd been. She'd never loved him. She hadn't even meant to start this. He was nothing to her but some untrustworthy gambler, good for nothing but scratching an itch.

"I know." Sadness filled those sweet green eyes. "I guess we've both made some pretty big mistakes."

"When?" he asked, the word sticking in his throat.

"When what?"

"When did you realize you were talking to me and not him?"

She blinked, then licked her lips. "Right before I came to your hotel. You said to come, and I didn't know it was you. I went to his condo."

Each word was like a drop of burning poison in his blood, but his desire to know the truth outweighed his need to protect himself from it.

Riley swallowed. "I found him with another woman, then you called and...everything kind of fell into place." She looked at the ceiling. "I was foolish enough to believe you wanted to be with *me*—me, not what I represent to the media. I was foolish enough to believe I was more to you that some publicity stunt."

"Riley—"

"Don't!" She shook her head. "I don't want to hear it, Charlie. I can't…"

I love you. She'd never intended those words for him, and he'd been carrying on as if they had been. "You love him."

She looked over her shoulder and back to Charlie. "No. Not anymore."

"And me?"

"No one else had access to that footage. No one else stood to profit from this. What am I supposed to think?"

"I guess that answers my question." He shook his head. "Goodbye, Riley. Enjoy your life. I hope you're satisfied, because there's a whole world out there you're too much of a coward to enjoy."

Hurt flashed in her eyes, but he was too angry to take it back.

TWENTY

CHAPTER

TWO

She'd hurt him.

Riley leaned her forehead on her knees and wondered why she cared so much about the man who betrayed her. The man who'd used her. After she'd gotten rid of Chaz, she hadn't moved from her spot on the couch, and she didn't have the physical or emotional energy to do so now. She'd been hollowed out.

Charlie said he loved her. How was that possible? How could he have given that press the video if he loved her? Had he really thought she'd believe he had nothing to do with it? Just yesterday he'd admitted to setting up the first pictures of them that had been released to the papers.

Her chest ached and her throat was raw, but more tears came.

The couch shifted under her.

"Lace," Riley said, reaching for her friend's hand. Lacey had found someone to cover her shift so she could be with Riley, and Riley had been grateful that she didn't have to be alone.

Lacey sat ramrod straight, frowning. "I just got off the phone with Charlie."

Riley withdrew her hand, another round of tears pressing against the back of her eyes. "I don't want to talk about your brother right now."

"You think he did it?" Lacey asked, her voice low and disbelieving.

Riley sniffed. "Who else? My father already talked to Griminski, and he swore he gave the only copy to Charlie. Griminski has worked for my father for a long time. I trust him."

"But you don't trust Charlie?" Lacey's mouth contorted in an ugly frown.

"If he didn't do it—" Riley took in a shaky breath, her eyes filling again.

"Of course he didn't do it," Lacey said. "Jesus, Riley, do you even know my brother?"

"Charlie 'the Devil' Singleton—yeah, I know all about him. I also know what his agent told him about needing a new sex scandal. And I know that he's responsible for the pictures the pap put in the paper. And I know that those pictures weren't enough to save his career. But this will be. Won't it?"

Lacey's only response was an angry tick in her jaw. Her hands gripped her knees.

"I'm trying to be reasonable," Riley explained. "Being naïve has gotten me nowhere."

Lacey stood and put her hands on her hips. "Do you even know *Charlie*, my brother, the man who loves you?" She shook her head. "Did you care about him at all, or was this just the rich girl having some wild fling with the bad boy?"

Riley gaped. "Lacey, I wouldn't…" She trailed off because she couldn't say anything. That was exactly what it had been. At least at first. "How was I supposed to know he wanted more?"

"You aren't the first rich bitch to use him like that, Riley. And you're not the first to take him at face value and assume there's nothing beneath the surface." Lacey dropped her hands and let out a breath, deflated. "You're just the first to surprise me."

Riley gaped, the ache in her chest growing. "Lacey, don't do this. I could really use a friend right now."

"Maybe *Chaz* would offer a shoulder to cry on. God knows he has the most to gain from this bullshit."

Riley squeezed her eyes shut, and thirty seconds later the front door slammed.

...

CHARLIE WANTED to lose himself in a bottle of bourbon, but he couldn't do that. Not when he had a tournament that began tomorrow. And not when there was someone he owed an apology.

Tony stood in his driveway, throwing a basketball into a rusty old hoop attached over the garage. He had a smooth rhythm. *Bounce. Bounce. Shoot. Swish. Bounce. Bounce. Shoot. Swish.*

"You're not bad at that," Charlie said after Tony made his fifth consecutive basket.

Tony turned to him, eyes wide. He tossed the ball, starting to walk away.

"It's Tony, isn't it?" Charlie asked, snatching the ball from the air.

Tony narrowed his eyes. "So what?"

Charlie shrugged. "My old man was never around." He eyed the basket, bounced the ball a couple times and shot. The ball bounced off the rim. "I made up stories about him when I was a kid—that he was away in the military, or that he was a secret agent."

The ball bounced on the pavement in front of Tony. "So?" he said, snatching the ball into a dribble.

"Then when I got older, I didn't make stuff up anymore," Charlie said as Tony lined up a shot. "I just hated him."

Those words threw Tony off at the last minute and his attempt went far left of its target.

Charlie took his chance and grabbed the rebound. "I never thought I'd be the absent father. I've been sexually active since I was your age, and not once did I fail to use protection."

Tony stepped in for the steal. With a quick twist, he jumped and the ball slid through the net. "I'm not stupid. I know last thing you want is some kid hanging around."

Charlie threw the ball across the yard. "Dammit, no one ever *asked* me what I wanted. I didn't plan to be a father, but that doesn't mean I didn't *want* you in my life."

Tony's eyes grew moist, and he turned away.

Charlie spun him around. "I wanted you. I just wasn't given the chance. I have the chance now."

"My mom says you're a bad influence. She grounded me when she found out I was going to play poker with you last night." Tears were rolling now. "Maybe she's right." He shook his head, sniffed, and wiped his face with the back of his hand. "Do you know how embarrassing it's going to be to go back to school in the fall after that video? All my friends have already seen it on YouTube."

Charlie felt his heart sink. He'd been in contact with his lawyer this morning and the video had already been pulled from the internet, but the damage was done. He clenched his hands to resist the urge to wipe away his son's tears. "I'm here to apologize," he said softly. "About the tape—I made a mistake, and I'm paying for it."

Tony nodded. "She is pretty hot," he said. He gave a half-shrug as if none of it mattered. "I can see how it could happen."

Charlie had to chuckle.

Tony's gaze dropped to the concrete. "I have a friend whose dad is involved with the tournament. He said there are rumors that you released the tape." Slowly, he lifted his head. "I told him you wouldn't do that. That rich lady, you love her, don't you?" He sniffed again. "It must be really hard to have people believe you'd sink that low for money."

Charlie wrapped his arms around Tony and pulled him against his chest. For a long moment, he closed his eyes, let himself appreciate the joy of having his son in his arms. "You should know there's a good chance I'll make a crappy father. I make mistakes sometimes, and I'm so far from perfect—"

"I don't need perfect."

"Thank you," he whispered.

"So, I guess you're going to be my dad now?" Tony said, pulling away.

Charlie smiled, his heart lightening. "I always was. Now I just have the chance to act like it."

"What are we going to do about Mom?"

Charlie followed Tony's gaze to the house and saw Angela standing in the window. Worry draped across her features and aged her ten years. "I'm going to make some changes, and I think she'll approve." Her gaze locked with his and he nodded in acknowledgement. "She'll come around."

Tony nodded. "I think so too. I think she's just afraid I'm going to drop out of school, but she should know I wouldn't do anything that stupid." His eyes darted to Charlie's. "No offense, man."

Charlie chuckled. "None taken. It was pretty stupid. If I had it to do over again—" He thought about his life, his impulsive youth, his poker career…Riley. She'd torn him apart inside but he couldn't imagine taking away his memories of her. He wouldn't give them up. "Well, I took a different path. But I wouldn't recommend it."

"Did you end up getting a sponsor for the Grand Escape tournament?"

Charlie sighed. Rick had been right, of course—sponsorship opportunities were flooding his phone since the footage broke. "I'll figure something out."

...

THE RECEPTIONIST on the twenty-second floor of the Grand Escape executive tower gave Charlie a disapproving frown, making him wonder if he'd have the pleasure of seeing a single person today who hadn't seen his ass on national television. "Ms. Carter isn't in today," she informed him.

Charlie dragged a hand through his hair and eyed the door to Quinton Carter's office.

"Excuse me. You can't go in there," the receptionist called as Charlie headed to the doors.

"I want to see him, Lettie!" Quinton boomed from his office.

Charlie pulled his shoulders back and prepared himself for battle.

He had met Quinton Carter several times but had never gotten over the impact of the man's presence in the room. In his stately office, piles of paperwork at either elbow, Quinton oozed importance. This was a man who had created an empire, a man who knew his value because he had manufactured it himself.

Without a doubt, this was a man who wouldn't want someone with Charlie's background anywhere near his daughter. But Charlie wasn't here about Riley.

Charlie entered and extended a hand. Quinton didn't stand or even offer his hand in return. "Mr. Singleton," he said by way of greeting.

"I appreciate you seeing me, sir. I only wish these weren't the circumstances."

Carter's only response was a raised brow. He was trying to be intimidating, and it worked.

"May I have a seat?"

Carter leaned back, crossing his arms over his chest. So, this was going to be a one-way conversation. So be it.

Charlie lowered himself into an upholstered chair facing the desk. "First I'd like to apologize for what happened with Riley." He shook his head. Quinton meant the world to his daughter, and Charlie wouldn't be the reason their relationship fell apart. "What I did was careless and impulsive, and I never intended for her to be hurt."

"Perhaps you should have considered that before you got under my daughter's skirt in a public, highly surveilled elevator."

Charlie swallowed, but his pride was thick and went down rough. "I agree, sir."

Quinton leaned forward and narrowed his eyes. "To come face to face with a girl's father after a video like that is released—that takes balls, son."

"I own up to my responsibilities."

"What about that child of yours?"

Charlie held Quinton's gaze. His talk with Tony had given him a strength he'd never felt before. "He's more than a responsibility. He's my son."

Quinton studied Charlie for a long moment. The tension ratcheted more tightly between them. "Why are you here, Singleton?"

"First, I think you should reinstate Griminski into his position.

He was trying to do something nice for me and it backfired. I hate to see a good man lose his job because of me."

"Griminski failed to follow a direct order. The decision made itself."

"Please, just...consider. He never would have done it if he'd known what would happen."

Quinton raised a brow. "And second?"

Charlie let the silence sit between them and prepared himself. "Second, you might know that I have yet to choose a sponsor for the Grand Escape Poker Tournament."

"You should have your pick, I'd imagine."

"With all due respect, sir, I have reservations about working with any company who thinks that video is a solid basis for a business relationship."

Quinton leaned back in his chair and gave Charlie a long, tedious once-over. "Why don't you tell me why you're really here, son."

Charlie nodded. "I have a business proposition for you."

TWENTY

CHAPTER

THREE

Cameras filled every corner of the room on the last day of the tournament. Charlie sat at the table with two remaining players, his eyes shielded by his customary sunglasses.

"All in," Charlie said without lifting the cards from where the dealer placed them before him.

Murmurs erupted around him.

Several feet from Riley, a commentator whispered into his microphone. "With what appears to be one reckless move after another, Charlie 'the Devil' Singleton has dominated play all week. His play has been too sporadic and unpredictable for us to determine whether he's truly apathetic or playing mind games."

Charlie slid his chips to the center of the table, and something deep inside Riley tugged viciously at her heart, trying to rip it away. She loved him. It was knowledge that had taken root and wouldn't go away.

One of the other two players at the table folded; the other pushed his chips to the center, matching Charlie's bet. Charlie didn't look at his cards even as the dealer showed the flop and the turn. Only after the river was laid face up did he flip his cards for himself and everyone around him to see.

Cheers erupted. "And the Devil wins it all!"

Charlie pushed his chair back and strode away from the table.

Riley slid back into the crowd so she could watch as he passed without him spotting her. She eyed the logo on his shirt: *Devil May Care Poker Clubs*. There was lots of buzz about the yet-to-be-opened Las Vegas poker clubs that had sponsored Charlie "the Devil" Singleton. Riley wondered how much they'd offered him. Not that it mattered.

She'd turned it over in her mind again and again, and Lacey was right. Charlie wouldn't have released that footage. And she was beyond foolish for believing otherwise.

She slipped from the crowd and made her way to the executive tower. She was on the stairs before she thought twice. Was Charlie right? Did she let her fears rule her life?

She finished the long ascent and went directly to Chaz's office.

Behind the polished mahogany desk, Chaz tapped at a keyboard and narrowed his eyes at the screen.

"Chaz."

He tapped a couple more times, leaned back in his chair, and smiled at her. The smile she once found warm and comforting sent a chill through her. "Hey, Riley."

Riley adjusted the strap on her shoulder as if her purse were a shield between them. "We need to talk."

He nodded to the chair facing him. "Have a seat."

"I'll stand, thank you."

"What happened to the sweet woman I used to know?" Chaz frowned and his eyes skimmed her, head to toe. "You've changed."

"I'll take that as a compliment."

He shook his head. "*He* did that to you—made you feel like you needed to change. I loved you the way you were."

"You loved the woman you could manipulate."

"Just because I'm not some freewheeling gambler who's sweet talking you…" He pulled a hand through his dark hair. "Just because I don't talk you into doing things in public elevators, and then, what? Watching the tape of it like some homemade porno? Jesus, Riley, what were you thinking?"

Riley closed her eyes. How had she been so stupid?

He sighed. "Maybe I need to do better. Maybe you're right, and I don't know enough about what you like outside this place. But I'm willing to learn. I love you."

She'd been so determined not to be the naïve little girl everyone assumed her to be that she'd blamed Charlie without consulting her heart. He was right. She was a coward. It had been easier to believe he'd done this than it had been to risk trusting him. "How do you know that Charlie and I watched the footage?"

Guilt passed over Chaz's features, turning them ugly for a moment before he caught himself. "Sweetheart, by now, everyone has watched it."

She shook her head. "That's not what you said and not what you meant. How would you know that Charlie and I watched the footage together?"

He stood and came around the desk, taking her hands in his and squeezing her fingers. There was no comfort in the contact. "I'm in love with you, Riley. Please, let's just start over."

"If you loved me, you wouldn't have given that video to the press."

Chaz narrowed his eyes and straightened. "So he's feeding you lies now? Who really stood to profit from that? Me or the poker player who's been losing his sponsorships for going soft?"

"I know you did it, Chaz, so don't try to pretend—"

His face grew hard and his hand gripped her wrist tighter. "Why? Why would I do that, Riley?"

"Because you knew I was falling for him. You knew you were going to lose me," she said. "And you want my father's company too much to let me go."

"I *didn't* want to lose you, and I haven't given up on you yet. But that's illogical." He shook his head. "See what I mean? He plants these ideas in your head. He's no good for you."

"He's the best thing that ever happened to me. He wanted me for *me*, not for my father's business, not for his money." And not for a publicity stunt. Only her insecurities had made her believe otherwise.

"I don't know what you're talking about."

Riley turned as her father entered the office, his broad shoulders and barrel chest filling the doorway. She'd called him on her way here, told him her suspicions, and asked him to make a few calls.

"Sir!" Chaz snapped to attention, hopping off the desk.

"Pack your things, Spencer. You're done. You won't be working for Carter Hotels and Entertainment anymore."

"That poker player is feeding her lies. Are you really going to let your daughter cavort with a—"

"Stop!" The word boomed from her father's mouth and filled the room, ricocheting off the walls. "I've spoken with your media connection. I know you were behind the footage. You're done."

Her father turned on his heel and left the office. Riley followed. "Thanks, Daddy."

He smoothed her hair back and pressed a kiss to the top of her head. "I should have seen him for what he is a long time ago."

She leaned into him. "He had us both fooled."

"What are you going to do about your poker player?"

She frowned. "I know you don't approve of him, but he was good for me. Better than I even realized, and if he would take me back, I'd go without a backward glance."

Her father raised a brow. "I never said I didn't approve, Riley. I just asked what you were doing." He smiled. "Anyone who makes you smile like that one did has all of my approval."

Riley's heart pitched. She wrapped her arms around her father and squeezed him tight. Charlie wouldn't be making her smile anymore, wouldn't be sweeping her off for romantic dinners or making her feel the shuffle of a thousand playing cards low in her belly. "I am glad he got a sponsor out of this mess. He's talented. He deserves a long career in poker." She withdrew and pulled her keys from her purse.

Her father frowned. "Charlie announced his retirement this afternoon."

Riley heard a clatter at her feet. She blinked down at the keys that had dropped to the floor. "Why would he do that?"

"He wants to be in Vegas fulltime to be near his son."

"Right. Of course."

"The Devil May Care Poker Club that sponsored him is mine—he agreed to be the face of a new set of poker clubs. And I couldn't beat the price for such good coverage."

"You opened a new set of clubs just for Charlie?"

He tucked a lock of hair behind Riley's ear. "That's the beautiful thing. Charlie suspected how much I hated owning strip clubs and suggested I turn the Black Diamond clubs into straight poker clubs."

Riley swallowed hard. It was a good idea. Poker clubs with Charlie's face would attract a lot of attention. Maybe not the kind poker clubs with naked women attracted, but these would be classier clubs where women would feel comfortable playing, where people could go who were looking for a serious game, not an excuse to stare at naked women. "It's genius," she said softly. "Is he going to run the clubs for you?"

Her father shook his head. "I offered, but he wasn't interested. He just wants an internship at Grand Escape while he works on his associate's degree in casino surveillance."

Some mix of pride and envy rushed through her. Pride that he'd had the courage to make a change, to pursue a new career. And envy for the same reason.

"I hurt him, Daddy. I don't know how to fix that. I was so wrong because I was scared to trust him."

"Have you told him that?"

She looked at her feet. "I'd like to, but I don't know if he wants to see my face right now."

Her father tipped up her chin and looked into her eyes. "He's only hurting so much because he loves you. He'll want to hear what you have to say."

"Do you know if he's left yet?"

"The after party is tonight. As the tournament winner, he'll be expected to be there."

Riley took a breath. It was Saturday. "I have something I have to do tonight, but I'll catch up with him tomorrow." She looked at her watch. If she was going to make it in time, she needed to head home for her things now. "I want you to know something, Daddy."

Her father rocked back on his heels. "What's that sweetheart?"

She bit her lip, caught herself, then lifted her chin. "I'm auditioning for a position in a dance company, and I know you don't approve, but you should know I'm not my mother and I won't be making the mistakes she did. You just have to trust me on that."

He sighed. "I trust you, Riley." Leaning forward, he kissed her forehead. "Knock 'em dead, sweetheart."

...

CHARLIE PULLED the last shirt off its hanger, folded it, and put it in his suitcase. Bright and early tomorrow morning, he'd check out of Grand Escape and head to Los Angeles to move out of his condo. Next time he returned to this hotel, it wouldn't be as a VIP guest but as an intern in training. The thought was terrifying and humbling. It was invigorating.

His phone buzzed. He grabbed it from the nightstand. *Text from Riley Carter.*

Something broke loose in his chest and sank, its ragged edges clawing the whole way down. He opened the text.

Come to the elevator.

...

RILEY SENT the text and darted into the elevator, white-knuckling her purse. She swiped her employee clearance card and jabbed the button for the penthouse, not allowing herself to wonder whether or not he wanted to see her.

The elevator started moving and she squeezed her eyes shut, swallowing the hot ball of fear threatening to spill from her gut.

The elevator dinged, and the doors slid open.

"Riley."

The image of Charlie before her was a kick in the chest, forcing her heart to double its pace. In jeans and a worn white oxford that hung unbuttoned and showed his tanned torso, he was every bit as sexy as the man her ING had spent years fantasizing about.

He stepped into the elevator with her and took her hand, pulling her gently toward the doors.

She gave a weak smile, but kept her feet glued where they were.

"It's okay, baby. I've got you. Come on."

Baby. Her heart warmed at that, but she shook her head. "I want to do this here. I'm not afraid." The doors slid closed behind Charlie and Riley flinched. "Okay, I am afraid—terrified—but I'm not letting that stop me."

"Okay." His dark eyes were cautious. Worried.

That warm kernel in her gut grew, moved its way up toward her heart.

"I'm so sorry I accused you of releasing that footage," she said softly. "I know you better than that, but I was scared."

Charlie let out a ragged breath. "I didn't give you any reason to believe I hadn't."

He stood stock still as she dropped her purse to her feet and slid her hands around his neck. "I love you, Charlie," she said. Then she pressed her lips to his.

She kissed him tentatively. After what she'd accused him of, he had every right to turn her away. But he didn't. Instead, he returned the kiss. She opened beneath him and slipped her tongue into his mouth, pressing her body closer to his.

Charlie's arms wrapped around her. One hand pulled at her hip, bringing her solidly against him. It wasn't until she moaned against his mouth that he pulled away. "I love you, Riley."

She smiled up at him. "I like hearing you say that."

He grinned. "Good. Because I like saying it." He brushed his lips against hers. "Are you sure you want to be with a washed-up old poker player who's enrolling in college for the first time at the age of thirty-two?"

She ran her thumb over the two-day growth of beard. He looked a little rugged and completely irresistible. "Sounds like the kind of guy who could teach me how to be brave and live my life for myself. Sounds like the kind of guy who could give me the courage to try out for a dance company."

He grinned. "Really?" At her nodded response, he leaned his

head against hers. "You are brave, Riley, and I never should have told you otherwise. Look at you. Right now. I've never known anyone so brave."

She swallowed. "I quit my job," she said. "I got a spot in Alysse's dance company, and I'm scared to death." She looked into his eyes as he stared down at her. "I'm really living for the first time since I was sixteen."

He pressed his lips to hers and she lost herself there again. Slipping a hand between their bodies, she found his bare chest, hot and hard beneath her fingertips. She moaned and he pulled away.

"As much as I hate to cut this short, we've been down this road before." He gave a meaningful look to the security camera over her head.

She grinned. "So what? Let them watch." And she kissed him again.

The End

If you enjoyed this book and would like to be notified when I release a new book, please sign up for my newsletter: http://eepurl.com/qymaH

Love Unbound by Lexi Ryan

Explore Love Unbound in Lexi Ryan's sexy and emotional books.

Love Unbound: Splintered Hearts
Unbreak Me (Maggie's story)
Stolen Wishes: A Wish I May Prequel Novella
(Will and Cally's prequel)
Wish I May (Will and Cally's novel)

Or read them together in the omnibus edition,
Splintered Hearts: The New Hope Trilogy

Love Unbound: Here and Now
Lost in Me (Hanna's story begins)
Fall to You (Hanna's story continues)
All for This (Hanna's story concludes)

Or read them together in the omnibus edition,
Here and Now: The Complete Series

Love Unbound: Reckless and Real
Something Wild (Liz and Sam's story begins)
Something Reckless (Liz and Sam's story continues)
Something Real (Liz and Sam's story concludes)

Love Unbound: Mended Hearts
Playing with Fire (Nix's story, coming summer 2015)

Other Titles by Lexi Ryan

Hot Contemporary Romance

Text Appeal
Accidental Sex Goddess

Decadence Creek Stories and Novellas

Just One Night
Just the Way You Are

Contact

I love hearing from readers, so find me on:

Facebook: facebook.com/lexiryanauthor
Twitter: @writerlexiryan
Email: writerlexiryan@gmail.com
Website: www.lexiryan.com